> **"Until the Immigration Department has finished its investigation, you need to share my room."**

Molly could not have said a word if her life depended on it. She was looking forward to the sanctity of her bedroom at night. A place where she could escape Kaliq's strong attraction and magnetism for a while each day.

"And when we're around others, we need to act like a devoted couple," Kaliq continued.

"What do you mean by 'devoted'?"

"Touching, smiling into each other's eyes like we hold the secret of the universe." He demonstrated, and Molly's knees went weak.

What would she give to have a man look at her like this and mean it? She'd always wanted to fall in love and get married. Instead, she'd fallen for the wrong man and married a different one.

And now not even her bedroom would be safe!

Dear Reader,

The year 2000 marks the twentieth anniversary of Silhouette Books! Ever since May 1980, Silhouette Books—and its flagship line, Silhouette Romance—has published the best in contemporary category romance fiction. And the year's stellar lineups across *all* Silhouette series continue that tradition.

This month in Silhouette Romance, Susan Meier unveils her miniseries BREWSTER BABY BOOM, in which three brothers confront instant fatherhood after inheriting six-month-old triplets! First up is *The Baby Bequest,* in which Evan Brewster does diaper duty…and learns a thing or two about love from his much-younger, mommy-in-the-making assistant. In Teresa Southwick's charming new Silhouette Romance novel, a tall, dark and handsome man decides to woo a jaded nurse *With a Little T.L.C. The Sheik's Solution* is a green-card marriage to his efficient secretary in this lavish fairy tale from Barbara McMahon.

Elizabeth Harbison's CINDERELLA BRIDES series continues with the magnificent *Annie and the Prince.* In Cara Colter's dramatic *A Babe in the Woods,* a mystery man arrives on a reclusive woman's doorstep with a babe on his back—and a gun in his backpack! Then we have a man without a memory who returns to his *Prim, Proper… Pregnant* former fiancée—this unique story by Alice Sharpe is a must-read for those who love twists and turns.

In coming months, look for special titles by longtime favorites Diana Palmer, Joan Hohl, Kasey Michaels, Dixie Browning, Phyllis Halldorson and Tracy Sinclair, as well as many newer but equally loved authors. It's an exciting year for Silhouette Books, and we invite you to join the celebration!

Happy reading!

Mary-Theresa Hussey

Mary-Theresa Hussey
Senior Editor

Please address questions and book requests to:
Silhouette Reader Service
U.S.: 3010 Walden Ave., P.O. Box 1325, Buffalo, NY 14269
Canadian: P.O. Box 609, Fort Erie, Ont. L2A 5X3

THE SHEIK'S SOLUTION

Barbara McMahon

Silhouette

ROMANCE™

Published by Silhouette Books

America's Publisher of Contemporary Romance

SILHOUETTE BOOKS

ISBN 0-373-19422-6

THE SHEIK'S SOLUTION

Copyright © 2000 by Barbara McMahon

Visit us at www.romance.net

Printed in U.S.A.

Books by Barbara McMahon

Silhouette Romance

Sheik Daddy #1132
The Sheik's Solution #1422

Silhouette Special Edition

Yours for Ninety Days #1282

Silhouette Desire

One Stubborn Cowboy #915
Cowboy's Bride #977
Bride of a Thousand Days #1017
Boss Lady and the Hired Hand #1072
Santa Cowboy #1116
*Cinderella Twin #1154
*The Older Man #1161
The Cowboy and the Virgin #1215

*Identical Twins!

BARBARA McMAHON

has made California her home since she graduated from the University of California (Berkeley) way back when! She's convinced she now has the perfect life, living on the western slopes of the Sierra Nevadas, sipping lattes on her front porch while she watches the deer graze nearby and playing "what if" with different story ideas. Even though she has sold over three dozen books, she says she still has another hundred tales to tell. Barbara also writes for Harlequin Romance. Readers can write Barbara at P.O. Box 977, Pioneer, CA 95666-0977.

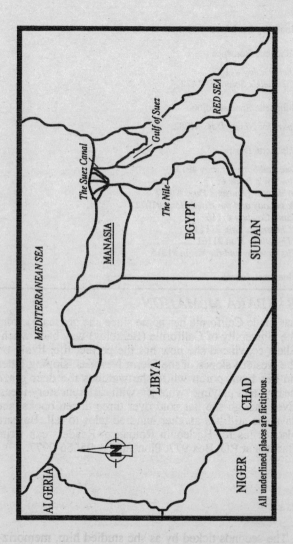

MEDITERRANEAN SEA

ALGERIA

LIBYA

NIGER

CHAD

MANASIA

EGYPT

SUDAN

The Nile

The Suez Canal

Gulf of Suez

RED SEA

N

All underlined places are fictitious.

Chapter One

Molly Larkin paused in the office doorway, holding a stack of files and letters. Her heart skipped a beat as she looked at her boss—Sheik Kaliq bin Shalik, though he rarely used his title in America.

She swallowed hard. He hadn't a clue she was watching him. As long as she was quiet, stood still, he wouldn't notice her. As usual, his concentration was fierce. He had the ability to tune out the rest of the world when he focused on one particular thing.

She loved looking at him. At his dark hair so meticulously styled—but often in disarray when he ran his fingers through it or came in from a windy day. At his dark straight brows, frowning now as he perused the spreadsheet. More than six feet tall, he stood a good seven inches above her own five-foot-six height. And every inch honed and taut as if he still rode the swift Arabian stallions of his homeland, not worked in a high-rise office building in Manhattan.

The seconds ticked by as she studied him, memorizing every detail. How many times in the five years she'd worked for him had she done this? More than a thousand, she knew.

And in two weeks she'd be gone, she thought with a pang. For a moment she almost faltered. *It wasn't fair!*

Studying the spreadsheet before him, Kaliq frowned as if he didn't like the totals. She wondered what he was reading—and didn't envy the writer. Kaliq was ruthless in business. Which accounted for his meteoric rise in the company—through sheer ability, not nepotism.

Sometime during the afternoon he'd discarded his suit jacket and loosened his tie. His shirtsleeves were rolled up, revealing his muscular tanned forearms. The snowy white shirt fit perfectly across broad shoulders before tapering to his waist. She couldn't see his eyes as he read, but their dark gaze never failed to cause a shiver down her spine.

He was a beautiful man, exotic and exciting in a way that had the office secretaries sighing whenever he walked by. But he was her boss, and Molly always kept that thought firmly in mind.

Besides, since the fiasco with Chad, she'd sworn never to become involved with another man. Once trust had been shattered, it was impossible to rebuild. She no longer had confidence in her judgment, her perception of others. And it would be a long time before she'd trust anyone again.

It was late. The rest of the staff had left for the weekend. Molly was ready to leave as soon as she gave Kaliq the folders. She allowed herself the indulgence of watching him for a little longer.

For a second she wondered how he would take her

resignation. He was a curious mixture of Western education and Middle Eastern tradition, making it very hard to gauge his reactions. Their company operated more formally than many in the United States, the style set by their boss with his manner of treating everything rather distantly. Did he ever lighten up? she wondered suddenly.

She'd never know.

Dusk was falling, visible through the large windows at his back. The scattered lights from the windows of the other skyscrapers sparkled. She'd seen this expanse of Manhattan every day for almost five years. It felt familiar, like home.

She smiled wryly. Kaliq would never approve of such blatant sentimentality. He was a tough no-nonsense businessman first, last and always. As he expected his personal assistant to be.

And if she had emulated him, she would never have found herself in the fix she was in now! Too bad she'd learned that lesson so late.

"I have the analysis you requested, and I brought the McCaffrey file, as well," Molly said, putting an abrupt end to her musing. "Elise finished the dictation you gave her, and those letters are on top. If you sign them now, I'll post them on my way out." Elise Templer had been Kaliq's secretary since before Molly started working for him as his personal assistant.

She placed the stack on his desk, relinquishing her own letter of resignation reluctantly. She didn't know what he was going to say, and hoped she could hold on to her control until she was alone. Resigning proved far more difficult than she'd expected.

He looked up and nodded, his dark eyes focused on her. "You read my mind about McCaffrey. I found a discrepancy in the latest numbers Hank reported. I need to compare them with our earlier report in their folder.''

She nodded with satisfaction. It had become almost a joke at first, when she'd started anticipating his needs. Over the past few years, however, they'd just accepted it as a part of their relationship. She knew the shipping business almost as well as he did, her ideas and thoughts usually paralleling his. And she always knew what information he needed almost before *he* knew.

''Does the merger still look promising?'' she asked, perching gingerly on the edge of one of the visitor's chairs opposite Kaliq. She let none of her impatience or trepidation show. He would get to her letter when he got to it.

Taking a deep breath, she held it a moment before letting it slowly out. It didn't calm her. So much for that theory.

Kaliq tossed down his pen and leaned back in his chair. ''Yes. Though the rate of return may not occur as quickly as I initially thought.''

He glanced at the stack, seemingly distracted.

Molly swallowed and waited patiently. She would not look at her watch again. Doing so would not change the pace of time.

Kaliq reached out and lifted the first of the letters, tilting it as he quickly read. When he finished, he scrawled his signature and tossed it aside, picking up the next. In only a couple of moments, he'd signed the lot.

He pushed the folders aside and spotted her letter. With a quick glance in her direction he picked up the envelope and withdrew the single sheet.

Molly studied him quietly as he read, vowing she

would not cry, even though she felt the threat of tears.
It was her decision, the only one she felt she could
make. But it hadn't come easily.

She owed Kaliq a great deal. She'd learned so much
from him. He'd talked her into taking night courses
until she got her degree, made sure she understood all
the regulations governing the shipping industry and
freely shared his own thoughts about the business. He'd
made her job interesting and exciting and rewarding.
She liked working with him despite the long hours and
the hectic pace he set. She would miss being his personal assistant. Miss living in New York.

Too late now for regrets. Months too late.

"What the hell is this?" He looked up right into her
eyes, his own narrowed.

She cleared her throat. "My resignation."

He stared at her for a long moment with the full
force of his dark eyes, then he slapped the paper down
and rose. Molly watched as he strode to the window
and gazed out over the busy street below. Leaning one
shoulder against the glass, he slipped his hands into the
pockets of his trousers.

As the silence stretched out, Molly's mind wandered.
She studied him, taking in the tall lean frame. Memorizing as much as she could. His clothes were made by
a London tailor. The dark somber colors and continen-
tal style did nothing to distract from his innate mas-
culinity, his dark good looks.

Should she say something? Try to explain?

That would be dumb. The entire reason for leaving
was to avoid explanations and excuses she knew would
result once people knew she was pregnant.

And deserted by the baby's father.

She couldn't endure the pity or the gossip. She had

to leave, and soon. Because at four months pregnant, the extent of her folly was about to be known.

Molly knew Kaliq would demand some kind of explanation. She shifted in her seat to gather up the signed letters, quickly folding them and inserting in the accompanying envelopes. Elise had made copies earlier. These were ready to be posted. She would drop them in the mail room before she left.

Glancing at her watch, she saw it was after seven. Still, someone was on duty in the mail room until eight. The letters would go out late, but at least they'd go out.

"Is there anything else you need?" she asked, longing to escape. Wishing she was already home. Wishing even more that she had not been put in this position at all! She didn't want to leave, yet felt she had no alternative.

"You could start by explaining that letter."

"I'm leaving New York," she said to his back.

"Going where?"

"I thought California." It was as far from New York as she could go.

He turned at that and stared at her in surprise. "Why? Joining some man?"

Heat stole into her cheeks and Molly looked away. "No. There is no man." Not now. And in reality, not ever. She'd been such a fool.

"Then why? I know your parents are dead. You have no other relatives, right? What the hell is in California?"

Startled, Molly looked up. Kaliq's dark brows were straight as he frowned. He rarely swore—at least not in her presence. He was angry. She recognized that instantly. She could practically feel waves of energy emanating from him—which was totally unlike the normally cool controlled man she'd worked with for so long. Businesslike and contained, that was Kaliq bin Shalik.

She'd always admired that. And had done her best to be the same way. To be the perfect personal assistant.

Did she owe him a full explanation? She hated to see the disappointment in his eyes. He didn't suffer fools gladly, and what she'd done was beyond foolish. Of course, he didn't have a very high opinion of women to begin with, thanks to his wife. Ex-wife, she corrected herself. So her own circumstances would only confirm that opinion.

When she'd started working for him, Kaliq had been married to a renowned British super model. But that union hadn't lasted long. Sabrina had been beautiful, elegant and sophisticated, but also greedy, conniving and unfaithful. He'd divorced her three years ago.

Since then, he'd played the field, never drawing close to any woman. And sometimes his remarks the day after a particularly trying date showed her clearly he didn't think highly of her gender.

"Is it something wrong with your work here?" he asked.

She shook her head. "I think it's time for a change. I need to leave New York." Rubbing her palms nervously against her long black skirt, she tried to remain calm.

"Leave New York? Why? Is it too expensive? Do you need more money?"

Molly flashed him an indignant look. "No, and if money were the issue, I'd list all I've done during the past year and let the record speak for itself."

He stifled a smile at her flare of temper. "You never used to speak up for yourself. You know your work is excellent. You don't miss anything, Molly."

Warmth spread through her. She smiled in genuine pleasure and wry amusement. He could have volunteered that information earlier. But it probably had never crossed his mind to do so.

He glanced at the letter again, a thoughtful expression on his face.

"I need to get this resolved," he said slowly. "Your timing couldn't be worse."

"There is nothing to resolve. I'm formally giving notice. I'll leave in two weeks."

"Do you have another job?"

"Not yet. I need to move and get settled first."

He crossed to the desk and leaned against it, looking down at her. "Tell me what's going on, Molly. You're moving across the country with no job, no family, nobody waiting. What's the deal? You owe me an explanation, don't you think?"

Did she owe any man anything?

Twisting her fingers, she looked at them, wondering what to do. She just wanted everything to go back the way it had been, but that would never happen. Everything was changing, out of control. She wondered if she could cope.

"I'm pregnant," she blurted out.

Silence.

She ventured a glance to find his dark gaze steadily on her.

"And the father doesn't live here in New York?"

"Oh, yes, he does," she said bitterly.

"Then why are you leaving?"

"Because he won't marry me!" She raised her chin,

drawing her pride around her like a cloak. "I don't want people to know how dumb I've been. I thought if I moved away, I could pretend to be a widow or something. No one would know my baby doesn't have a father willing to acknowledge it."

"Good grief. Isn't that a bit drastic? Moving away from your friends, your job? You wouldn't have any kind of support network."

"I can manage. I've saved some money, and I know I can get another job."

"Single women have babies all the time. You don't need to move clear across the country," he snapped.

"Maybe single women have babies, but it's considered tacky to be an unwed mother in my hometown. Small towns in Ohio frown on that kind of thing. And I didn't realize how much stuck. I've lived here for years, but still feel...I don't know, embarrassed, I guess, is the least of it. And a certain amount of shame. I'd hate for my baby to know his daddy didn't want him. Or her."

"So you plan to keep the baby?"

Molly nodded. It was odd. With all the anger she felt toward Chad, she thought that some of it would have transferred to the baby, that she might even come to resent the child. But she already loved this infant growing beneath her heart.

Molly had no family. Once her baby was born, it would be just the two of them against the world. The thought of that precious new life was the only bright spot in her day. Despite the complications an unexpected pregnancy brought, she was looking forward to holding her baby.

"Who's the father?"

"Just a guy."

"I don't buy that, Molly. You aren't the type for casual sex. Who is he? That Chad you've been quietly dating for a year or so?"

She shrugged, a bit annoyed by the inquisition. Then nodded.

"I thought he was wonderful. Bright, funny, charming. I really liked being with him. I thought I loved him. He said he loved me. But I know better now. I'll never trust a man again!" Or her own judgment. She'd felt sure she was loved. How could she have been so wrong?

"He heard about the baby and left?" Kaliq guessed shrewdly.

"Two months ago."

"Want me to track him down and make him marry you?"

She widened her eyes. Kaliq could do it if anyone could. Slowly she shook her head. "No. In the first place, I wouldn't marry him now if he were the last man on earth. Not that I could. He's already married—has been for years. A minor little detail he conveniently forgot to mention to me. I was just on the side, so to speak."

Tears threatened as she remembered how ashamed she'd felt when Chad had told her the cold hard facts. How ashamed and scared and furious.

"Molly—"

She jumped up. "Don't say anything, Kaliq. I know I was an idiot. But you don't have to worry I'll repeat that dumb mistake. I have to do what's best for me and my baby, and staying here isn't an option. I've really enjoyed working with you." Backing toward the door, she tried to keep a bright smile on her face, but from her trembling lips, she knew she was failing.

Kaliq watched Molly as she bid him good-night. His gaze continued to follow her as she entered the outer office. Her thick chestnut hair caught back in a long ponytail at the base of her neck was tidy, even after a full day at work. She always appeared immaculate. Slender, perhaps too slender, she dressed conservatively. Mostly in black and silver, he noticed. Today her black skirt swayed seductively against her long legs as she walked away. It hit her midcalf, a softly feminine garment. Her silvery blouse had been fastened to within two buttons of the neck, but displayed the generous curves that enhanced her femininity. The gold that nestled against her throat warmed the honey tones of her skin. Beautiful, confident, poised—he admired all those features in his personal assistant.

Almost as much as he admired her business acumen.

She didn't look pregnant. How far along was she? Surprised at the turn of events, he shook his head. Timing was everything—and he'd just been dealt a second major blow.

Never in all the years she'd worked for him had Molly been anything but totally professional. He'd taken her for granted, he realized. She'd been the perfect personal assistant. He couldn't even remember their first few months together, but he knew they must have been awkward. There had been so much for her to learn. But she'd caught on faster than anyone he'd ever worked with.

Molly had quickly become invaluable to him. Since talking with the legal department, he'd wondered if Molly could prove equally valuable to the company—managing it in his absence?

He frowned, not even wanting to imagine giving into the inevitable. He had time, a week at least.

Frustrated with the turn of events, he moved back to his desk. He came from a family with strong loyalty, unbreakable family ties. How could a man betray his wife by having an affair? And then betray someone like Molly? His own family was large but close. He'd do anything for them. They had only to ask.

Kaliq often felt Molly would do the same for him, which was rare in employees these days. Was her loyalty to the company or to him alone? Could he find a way to keep her on board? If his own situation didn't improve, this would be the worst time for her to leave.

Her resignation was not an option. He had to convince her to stay. To hell with what people thought. She was a colleague, a close confidante, as well as an employee. Her departure would end that. Kaliq refused to even consider the idea.

He didn't need this added problem. The documents delivered earlier reclaimed his attention. His visa had expired. Someone on the legal staff had screwed up and not applied for the extension when it was time. Now he had to figure out how to fight deportation.

He was in the midst of negotiations for new contracts with the longshoremen's union. Had just finalized the buyout of a small domestic shipping line. Merging that into the parent company would also take time, and his own skills. He could not afford to be gone for a week, much less the months it might take for him to return home and wait for a new visa to be processed.

He was not giving up. It would just take thought and strategy to address the problem.

Hearing a noise in the outer office, Kaliq looked up. *Molly.*

Damn, he was slow today.

Why hadn't he thought of her immediately? He quickly crossed to the door.

Molly had gathered her purse and the tote that held her dress shoes. She'd already changed into low walking shoes for her trip home.

"Did you need something?" she asked.

"Come back in for a moment, Molly. I may have an answer to our problems—yours and mine." He waited until she'd placed her things on the desk and walked toward him before continuing. "Yesterday I was served notice by Immigration. My visa expired some time ago, and Phil Mannering in legal neglected to make sure it was renewed. I'm being deported to Manasia."

Molly appeared stunned. "Can they do that? You run this place. Can't you get an extension or something?"

"Apparently your federal law is such that citizens in my country need to be living there when applying for a new visa. Since the old one expired, I am required to apply for a new one. Had the current visa been extended, I wouldn't be in this fix."

"How long does that take?" she asked.

"At least several months. Maybe longer. I don't know where the United States stands with quotas from Manasia. I've had that visa for so long I don't even remember all I had to go through to obtain it initially. And who knows how much more red tape there is now in that massive bureaucracy."

"Can't Roeuk help? Doesn't he have some pull in Washington?" Kaliq's cousin, Roeuk bin Shalik, visited the United States for several months every year. His wife and daughter had once lived in Washington,

D.C., and now his family split their time between their two homes.

"I called him as soon as I found out. He's looking into it. But unless something comes up quickly, it'll be too late. I'm scheduled to depart next Friday."

Molly leaned against the doorjamb and stared at him, her mind whirling as she wrestled with the problem. For the moment the challenge reminded her of countless other times they had hashed out impossible situations. This was serious.

"I don't know what to say. I know nothing about immigration laws and procedures."

"I believe I've come up with the perfect solution," he said easily. Kaliq looked just like he did when making a huge coup in business—arrogantly confident, supremely assured and a bit like the cat who swallowed the canary.

"Marry me," Kaliq said.

"What?" The room seemed to whirl around, then dimmed. For a moment Molly thought she might faint. Only the pull of Kaliq's dark eyes held her, anchored her.

Was she hallucinating? Had he just asked her to *marry* him?

He stood close enough she could see the depth in his eyes, notice the fine lines that radiated from the corners.

"At least consider it before raising objections," he said. "I haven't worked out all the details—we can do that together. But I believe this will work. You would not be an unmarried mother and I would make sure you didn't go through this pregnancy alone. You'd be my wife until I obtain permanent residency. Longer if it works out. We can each provide the other something we need."

She shook her head, unable to tear her gaze from his. Her heart pounded, and she tried to think. But her emotions threatened to overwhelm her. Kaliq wanted to *marry* her? As in kisses and living together and—

"It's our answer," Kaliq said. "You wouldn't have to quit your job. You can continue to work as long as you feel like it."

"And after? When the baby is born and you have your residency, then what?" Amazed that her voice sounded so normal, Molly still leaned against the doorjamb.

"We'll see how things go. We can get a quiet divorce. I'll make sure you are adequately situated financially."

"I don't need your money," she said hotly. Did he think he could buy a wife? That she was so desperate she'd consider such a move?

He nodded. "Fine, then. I'll establish a small trust for the child."

"It won't work," she said. The last thing she wanted to do was depend on a man for anything. Too much could go wrong with this idea. Just thinking about it had her heart racing, her knees wobbling. She couldn't possibly consider marrying Kaliq.

She wasn't sophisticated like the women he usually dated. And before much longer she would be as big as a house. Was he seriously proposing that she become his wife to save him from deportation? There must be fifty thousand women in New York City alone who would jump at the opportunity.

"Why me? Why marriage?"

"A marriage of convenience is not unheard-of even

in this country,'' he replied. "People marry for expediency all the time. It is not at all uncommon to find arranged marriages in my country. Often the families of the couple arrange the alliance. A marriage based on mutual respect and common interest will work, Molly. On paper we'll be married, and in reality little will change. You'll continue to work as my personal assistant as long as you can. After the baby is born, we will separate, sever the legal tie. But I'll keep your job for you."

"You can't marry just because you don't have a current visa," she protested, dazed at the thought. Though wary at his suggestion, the idea held strong appeal. She wouldn't be an unwed mother. Wouldn't have to worry about gossip and feeling shame and moving clear across the country when she really loved New York. She wouldn't have to leave Kaliq or her job.

His features tightened slightly. He narrowed his eyes. "I wish to remain in America. To leave for even a few months would be inconvenient. The idea has further appeal—I attend many functions during the year, and it's awkward to go alone all the time. And if I wish to reciprocate, I need a hostess. So you see, it would benefit me in other areas to have a wife."

She stared at him. Realization gradually seeped in. Here was another man barreling through life at her expense, just as Chad had. Kaliq wanted a marriage in name only, not because he cared for her, but for his convenience.

But what about *her* convenience?

He tilted his head, watching her. "What's your answer?"

"I have a choice?" she asked. She should stick with her original plan.

Only…the thought of relocating was overwhelming. It would be far easier to stay where she was, have adequate help while she needed it, keep the job she loved.

"You may decline," Kaliq said, his expression giving nothing away.

The coolness in his tone let her know he would not be pleased if she refused.

Another thought flashed through her mind—if she didn't marry him, he would likely turn to someone else. Which would leave Molly no choice but to move.

Or you could stay.

Why not accept? she thought frantically. Chad had proved how fickle love could be. She didn't plan to ever become involved again. She'd make her career the most important thing in her life—after her baby. Would marrying Kaliq help in that regard? Probably. So why not a temporary marriage of convenience?

"What about my baby? Would you truly be willing to let people think it's yours? What about when we divorce?" She was surprised at how calm she sounded. Maybe he couldn't hear the pounding of her heart, the blood thundering through her veins, almost drowning out her own voice.

"The baby is yours. While we are married, I will not repudiate it. Nor, however, can I make it my heir. When we separate, I'll provide for the child. I believe that is more than fair."

She nodded. He must really want to remain in the States to give so much to another man's child.

What was she thinking? They had nothing in common! He was Arabian royalty, a member of the ruling house in Manasia. She was the daughter of a small-town banker. Was he mad?

Or was she to even consider saying yes?

Just then she felt a fluttering deep inside. The baby was moving again. She wasn't alone anymore. She had her child. And needed to do the best she could for that child.

"This arrangement will suit us both," he went on. "I think Americans have a peculiar romantic view of love and living happily ever after. Arranged marriages often prove extremely successful. I believe this choice is better than your plan. You're what—twenty-seven?"

"Twenty-eight." Her birthday was three months ago and he never acknowledged it, she thought wryly. Would anything change with a marriage license between them?

"A bit old to uproot yourself on the chance of finding a good job on the West Coast. Stay here where you can continue living the life you've made for yourself."

"Would I keep my job when we annul the marriage?"

"We work well together. I see no reason to change that."

He crossed to his desk and riffled through his appointment calendar. "If I get Elise to reschedule some of next week's appointments, we'll have time to get married and notify Immigration before Friday. I'll have Mannering get to work on everything first thing Monday." He looked up. "Does that suit you?"

"I'm not sure this is such a good idea." There was no way she could marry Kaliq bin Shalik. Why was she even discussing the matter?

His gaze caught hers, but he kept silent, as if the sheer force of his personality could convince her. The effect almost knocked what little sense Molly possessed right out of her head. He looked incredibly assured, determined, sexy.

Sexy?

She *was* losing her mind. The last thing she wanted was involvement with another man. She'd learned that lesson well. This had to be a case of spiking hormones!

He studied her for another moment. "At least I know up front you're not marrying me for my money or with some false declarations of my undying love. That will save a lot of heartbreak later."

"I never said I'd marry you at all," she protested. How like the man to just declare what he wanted and assume she would fall in with his plans. Swallowing hard, she tried to focus on the possibility. It proved impossible.

"So say it and end the suspense. I don't have a lot of time here, Molly."

She swallowed again and opened her mouth. Then shut it. Sanity took over. She needed some time to consider his outrageous idea, no matter how short he was on the commodity.

"I need to think this through," she said. Would he kiss her as her husband? Expect more from her than she could give? Or would it be a paper marriage only? Just an appeasement for Immigration?

And a way to save face for her?

That alone should have her leaping at the chance.

He nodded. "I can understand that. Until Monday, then."

Molly hesitated, wishing he'd say something else, something that gave her a clue as to what would truly be their best course. But he seemed to have accepted her request and already turned his attention elsewhere as he picked up the spreadsheet in front of him and began to review the numbers.

Molly left, still feeling dazed and disoriented. She couldn't concentrate on anything except the echo of Kaliq's words, *Marry me.*

Chapter Two

Molly slept very little that night. She tossed and turned, tried to consider all the ramifications of marrying her boss compared to those of not marrying him. It was a futile endeavor. She couldn't keep a coherent thought straight for more than ten seconds. Her mind spun. She'd been committed to moving for weeks, ever since she'd finally admitted to herself that Chad was not going to do anything to help her. She'd started packing, had lined up a moving company, told her roommate she'd be gone by the end of the month.

Now she was supposed to consider an alternative.

She tried to envision life as the wife of Kaliq bin Shalik, but simply couldn't. She didn't have the background or training to move in his exalted circles. Couldn't imagine living with him away from the office. Exchanging personal information.

Yet the thought was tantalizing. He'd fascinated her for years.

She wouldn't expect Kaliq to take on the role of

doting father. But his willingness to let others believe the child was his touched her.

She wouldn't mind the rest—later. Divorced mothers were everywhere. When it came time, she could manage that. At least she thought she could. And there was always California.

But was she being fair to Kaliq? She would reap more from this temporary marriage than he would. He could put up with the inconvenience of waiting a few weeks while a new visa was being processed. Did he have to marry? Weren't there other better alternatives for him?

Finally giving in to her restlessness, she rose and took a long shower. Dressed in faded jeans and a snug top, she brushed her hair until it shone, then pulled it back into her normal neat ponytail. Dressed for a day at home, she headed for the kitchen.

Though she longed for coffee, Molly dutifully drank herbal tea, instead. She could no longer consider only her own wants and needs, she had to make sure the baby was taken care of properly. Preparing a couple of slices of toast, she loaded on the strawberry jam and sat down.

Drawing a pad from the counter, she sketched a chart and began to list the pros and cons of Kaliq's unexpected proposal.

But concentration continued to prove impossible. All she could think of was his dark gaze. The shimmering feeling of anticipation that seeped into her every cell when he turned those dark eyes on her.

She attempted to picture him sitting opposite her at the breakfast table.

Impossible.

She closed her eyes and tried to envision herself on

the social whirl. He attended opening nights and special showings at the museum and art galleries. His cadre of friends included the heads of many major companies and some English aristocracy. What would she talk about to people like that? She was terrible at small talk. Business discussions, okay, or even girlish confidences she could handle—but nothing suitable for the circles Kaliq moved in.

Shaking her head, she finished her meager breakfast and wandered into the living room. Her roommate was away this weekend. Susan was trying so hard to be supportive, but she really hadn't come up with a strong plan to convince Molly to stay. What would she say to Kaliq's bizarre proposal?

She'd still be moving from the apartment. Her heart skipped a beat when she wondered what his home looked like. Then a kaleidoscope of images flashed through her mind's eye, ending up with him drawing her into his arms and kissing her.

Omigod, she thought, *what will I do if he kisses me?* Which he probably would at the wedding ceremony, at least. Wasn't that part of the ritual?

Flushing, Molly wondered why she fixated on a possible kiss. There were a million other things to think about.

She checked the clock. It wasn't even eight. Pacing the small room, she tried to make sense of her tumbled thoughts. She couldn't. Maybe she'd go talk to the man. Get everything straight, understand exactly what their marriage would entail. Then maybe she could make the right decision.

That decided, she wasted no time. If he wasn't at the office yet, she knew he'd be there before long. But when she signed in, she saw Kaliq's name boldly written two lines above. He was already here.

Swallowing her trepidation, she turned to the elevators. It was only on the ride up that she realized she was wearing jeans that had seen better days, scuffed running shoes and a top that had been designed more for comfort than style.

"Just shows I'm not thinking straight," she murmured in the empty car.

When it opened on her floor, she hesitated. Maybe she should return home and think this through a bit more.

And change her clothes.

She ignored that thought, then stepped out and quickly made her way to her office. If she went home, she might lose her courage. Dropping her purse on her desk, she didn't pause but continued to Kaliq's door. It stood ajar. No need to shut it for privacy when he was the only one here.

"Kaliq?" she said.

He looked up, laid his pen down and let his gaze travel from her face slowly down her body and back up again. Molly almost squirmed when he seemed to linger on her breasts and the snug fit of her top. She definitely should have changed.

"I didn't expect to see you today. Come in." He rose politely.

For a moment Molly hesitated. His proposal still echoed. For once she didn't see him as her boss—but rather as the man she might marry. He would be her husband!

Stepping into his office, Molly felt decidedly underdressed compared with his dark slacks and dress shirt. Granted, he wore no tie, the collar buttons were undone and the sleeves rolled up, but still, didn't the man ever relax and wear casual clothing?

She cleared her throat nervously and tried to smile, then gave up. Crossing swiftly to the visitor's chair, she dropped into it and stared at him.

"I've given your suggestion some thought," she began, wishing she could clear the sense of desperation that gripped her.

He nodded and sat, his eyes focused on her. "And?"

"I would like some more information. I think we need to discuss this further."

"Information such as?"

"How you expect such an alliance to work," she blurted out. So much for the carefully rehearsed speech she'd practiced in the cab.

He leaned back in his chair, his gaze never leaving hers. "I expect we'll get along fine. We have for five years."

"I meant, precisely how do you see this working? Would I keep my apartment? Visit your place when you wanted to hold a party or something? Move in with you right away?" *Share a bed?* That she couldn't voice, not yet.

He shook his head. "Our arrangement must appear to be a normal marriage in every regard, Molly. We have to convince your government that this is real. We'll be interviewed and questioned by the Immigration and Naturalization Service. INS will want to inspect our living arrangements. You'll have to give up your place and move into mine. If you don't like my apartment, we can look for something together that would suit us both. It's imperative that we convince Immigration that this is a true and lasting marriage. I understand they frown on foreign nationals making marriages just for the sake of remaining in the United States.''

"Which this would be.''

"As long as we give the appearance of a normal marriage, I doubt there will be any challenges. In fact, your pregnancy could work strongly in my favor. No one would question a hurry-up wedding if the bride is already pregnant.''

She nodded—especially if they didn't bother to name the real father. She kept her personal life private. No one knew she'd been dating Chad except her roommate. She cleared her throat, wishing she had typed up a list of questions. Her mind spun, but no coherent thoughts seemed to come through. At last she spoke.

"You said a normal marriage. Normal, how? Like cooking and cleaning the apartment and shopping?''

Like sleeping together, kissing, making love?

She longed to ask about every aspect, but shyness kept her tongue silent. She was not looking for normal in any sense. Her lesson had been hard-learned, but permanent.

"I don't need a cook or maid. I have a man now who looks after the apartment. I see no reason Hasim wouldn't continue his duties just because you'll be living there.''

She nodded. What else was there?

"I have some furniture that belonged to my parents,'' she said. "I'd like to bring that.''

"Of course. It will be your home, so do with it what you will.''

"And I have lots of friends. I don't want to change that because of a new husband.''

Although, until yesterday, she had planned to cease her friendships except for a few very close ones. She hated the thought of everyone knowing the circumstances surrounding her baby.

"I would not expect you to change your life drastically. My home would become your home. You would be free to invite whomever you wished to visit us."

"I'm not good at social chitchat," she said slowly, her mind still spinning. He countered her every worry. Was she seriously considering the proposal?

A hint of amusement crept into Kaliq's eyes. "Neither am I, truth be told. I much prefer the working environment. But duty does necessitate social obligations. Especially when dealing with business rivals, clients and vendors. It makes the entire process run more smoothly. You'll do fine, Molly. You're polished and sophisticated...." His voice trailed off as he glanced at her worn jeans.

She grimaced. "Fooled you, Kaliq. This is me when I'm not working. I'm not into fancy dresses and lots of jewelry. I prefer jeans and comfortable tops. I'm not all that sophisticated or polished even after five years in New York. I clean up good. But my jeans are already getting tight. And in another few months I'll be pretty big."

And on her best days she never looked like a super model.

"I like what you're wearing," he said.

"You do?" He astonished her.

"You hide your body in those clothes you normally wear. Now its shape is revealed. And a very nice sexy body it is, too. Very appealing."

She froze. The last thing she wished was to appear appealing. She wanted no attraction between them. This proposed marriage was for expediency only—

nothing more. Color flushed her cheeks, and Molly dropped her gaze to the polished surface of his desk. Tingling sensations skipped along her nerves. He'd never given a hint he'd noticed her as a woman. She was his personal assistant—being married would not change that.

"You're a lovely woman, Molly. I believe that we will suit each other well, or I would not have made the offer. Pregnant women usually seem quite beautiful. And we can afford to obtain the latest in haute couture for any stage of pregnancy. Have I answered your concerns? Is there anything else?"

"Sex," she blurted out before she could think.

"Ah. For or against?" He didn't seem the least bit perturbed.

She glared at him. How dare he be so casual? Was he teasing?

Blood thundered through her veins again, heating her body. Making love with Kaliq? She had never been one for casual sex. She had thought herself in love with Chad—only to discover how false that proved. She could never sleep with a man who viewed her as part of a business deal. Did Kaliq wish to make this temporary marriage normal in every respect? She needed to know before making a final decision.

Definite amusement lurked in his eyes, which surprised her. She hadn't expected that. Molly wished she could be inspired with some scathing putdown that would erase that mocking glint and put her back on an equal footing. But she could only feel the tumultuous emotions that threatened to overwhelm her.

"Perhaps that is a topic we could discuss at some length later," he said smoothly when she didn't answer.

"I would keep my job?" she asked, glad to change the subject.

"Of course. You are the best personal assistant I've ever had. As I told you, one of the reasons I proposed this plan was to keep from losing you."

"Okay, then, I guess I'll marry you."

Kaliq actually laughed. "You are good for keeping a man's ego in line. I bet condemned prisoners sound more enthusiastic. But I thank you. I will endeavor to make sure you never regret your kindness."

"Um, I'll guess we'll see as time goes on, won't we?" She rose. "Bye."

"Where are you going?"

"Today's Saturday. Unlike you, I do not plan to spend it at work. I have places to go and things to do."

"Such as?" He rose and moved around the desk in that lithe grace she suddenly found fascinating.

Don't come any closer, she thought, panicking, *or I'll lose my train of thought.* But he obviously couldn't read minds, because he stepped right up beside her.

Molly breathed in the scent of his aftershave. Spicy and masculine, it called forth a small fire deep within. What was wrong with her? She'd been closer to him many times and never had this reaction before.

"Um..." She looked away and tried to think of some activity that would satisfy his curiosity.

When Kaliq reached out to brush an errant strand of hair from her cheek, she jumped. Her gaze flying to his, Molly held her breath. In all the years she'd worked for him, he'd never touched her.

And a good thing, too. Shimmering excitement danced along her cheek as the feel of his warm fingertips lingered. She searched his eyes for any sign he'd felt something when he touched her.

His oblique gaze revealed nothing. Impassivity was fine when dealing with longshoremen, but Molly would have liked some indication of what Kaliq was feeling. Was she the only one to notice that spark?

"If you have prior obligations, then do not let me detain you," he said. "Thank you for agreeing to become my wife. We will see to the arrangements on Monday."

Kaliq reached for her hand and clasped it lightly in his, then lifted it and turned it palm up. Lightly he brushed his lips across her wrist. "You do me great honor in your agreement," he said in his husky voice with the slight British intonation.

"It is I who am honored," Molly replied, still feeling the warmth his light caress engendered. "I'll make sure my baby never does anything to sully your family name."

He smiled slightly and leaned closer.

Pulling her hand free, Molly turned and fled. She snatched up her purse in passing and hurried to the elevator. The car she'd come up in was still on the floor, so she instantly stepped inside and punched the button for the lobby, leaning against the side wall, willing the doors to close swiftly.

She tried to get her roiling emotions under control. She was engaged to Sheik Kaliq bin Shalik! And he'd sealed their bargain with a kiss.

Not on the mouth as she might have expected, but a kiss, nevertheless. One she could still feel. If she hadn't run like a scared rabbit, would he have given her a real kiss?

Molly turned right from the building entrance and began walking briskly in an attempt to escape her thoughts. She couldn't believe she'd just agreed to marry the man. She still had a dozen questions, a dozen concerns. But it was too late—she'd said yes.

With an odd sense of elation, Kaliq watched Molly practically run from the office and head for the elevators. Slowly he turned and moved to the windows. It was sunny and warm outside, but the climate control of the building gave little hint of the balmy weather. He wondered where Molly was heading in such a hurry. The offices were too high for him to see her when she emerged from the building, but he watched the pedestrians, anyway.

He knew little about his assistant beyond how well she worked for him. Who were her friends? How had she gotten mixed up with a married man? If the signs were anything to go by, she was hurt, afraid and doubly wary now.

Which suited him. Their marriage was a business deal. When the crises had passed, they could each resume their normal lives. He didn't want her imagining she was falling in love.

From this moment on, however, she was his—temporarily.

A peculiar feeling of satisfaction filled him. He had been surprised at her visit this morning, and intrigued to see her in clothes that were so different from the attire she usually wore to work. He liked her top. Its snug fit displayed her figure to advantage. She was stunning.

The softness of her skin had been another surprise. Had she not pulled away so abruptly, he would have kissed her again, moving this time to that inviting mouth that seemed to cry for his attention this morning. How could he have overlooked it in the past?

Would she be shy and wary in her kisses? Or bold and daring?

Impatient with his thoughts, he turned back to his desk. There were a few more items he wished to cover today. Monday, he would have Elise clear his calendar for the week, except for the longshoremen's contract negotiations, which wouldn't wait. He wanted to be prepared for every demand and be able to back up his counteroffers with as much data as possible.

But just before he pulled the analyses from the folder, he looked through the door to where Molly usually sat. He almost wished he'd been going with her today—wherever she was going.

Time enough when they were married to do things together. They had not discussed that possibility. He looked forward to Molly's reaction when he brought it up.

When Molly stepped off the elevator Monday morning, she was instantly surrounded by fellow workers wishing her well. Kaliq had obviously wasted no time in letting the entire firm know of their pending nuptials.

"Thank you." She smiled politely as two secretaries wished her happiness, then bombarded her with questions.

"So, tell us how it happened?"

"When did he propose?"

"Isn't he the most romantic man you know?"

"Where are you going to live?"

"Will you keep your job?"

Molly looked at Monique. The young woman had worked for them seven months. She was competent, but not at all satisfied with her job. Ambitious, she had yet to prove herself ready for additional responsibility.

Sometimes Molly thought the woman just wanted more money.

"Did you get your ring yet?" With a glance of disappointment, Shelly looked at her left hand, then brightened. "Oh, I know, you'll shop for it together."

"Not likely," Monique interrupted. "I'm sure Kaliq has a fortune in jewels in the family vault." She waved her hand vaguely. "He probably sent for them to present to his future wife. I imagine they're worth a small fortune. Won't you be worried wearing thousands of dollars' worth of jewels around here?"

Molly shook her head, slowly making her way toward her office. She needed to speak to Kaliq. Smiling, she tried to appear the happy fiancée and answer all their questions. The last thing either she or Kaliq wanted was suspicions.

"I don't know anything about jewels. We'll get things sorted out soon, and I'll let you all know. In the meantime I have work to do, and I suspect you all do, as well. Excuse me."

Elise smiled sympathetically when Molly reached her desk. "Sorry, I think it was my fault. When Kaliq told me, I was so surprised and delighted that I called Betty in personnel. She is a bit of a blabbermouth."

Molly rolled her eyes and nodded. "You've got that right. Please, tell everyone I really appreciate their interest, but we do have work to do."

"Including my new assignment, find out all I can about instant marriages in New York. If I can't get the answer soon, Kaliq's threatening to fly out to Las Vegas tomorrow and marry you there."

"Great, just what I always wanted, a wedding with an Elvis impersonator officiating." Molly crossed the room to her desk and wondered what it would be like to be so wildly in love with a man they were both impatient to get married. Like she thought she and Chad might have been several months ago. In such an event, maybe even an Elvis wedding at some tacky chapel in Las Vegas would be worth it.

But this marriage was a business deal, one Kaliq was obviously planning to finalize as soon as possible to stall the INS. A quiet ceremony at City Hall would be much more his style.

For a moment Molly gave a thought to a traditional wedding. Since her parents had died in a plane crash when she was fourteen, Molly had never really planned on a formal traditional wedding. She wondered if her father had once longed to walk her down the aisle. If her mother had wanted Molly to wear her wedding dress. Had they not died, Molly probably would still be living in Ohio and would never have met Kaliq.

If she and Chad had married, maybe she would have opted for a formal ceremony in memory of her parents. But Kaliq's family didn't live in America, and she suspected he was not inviting them.

In fact, she wondered if he would even tell them. There was no need. The marriage would be over in a few short months—and it wasn't as if it was real.

"Good morning, Molly," Kaliq said, coming out of his office. "I expect Frank LeBec to arrive in about ten minutes. We'll be reviewing some of the demands from the union. I have Phil and Josh joining us, and I want you to sit in on the meeting, as well. Elise has the conference room set up. Anything you think I should know about LeBec? You've met him before—I haven't."

"He's a bit belligerent because of his lack of formal education, I've always thought. He had to drop out of

school to help his family when he was a teenager, and
as he moves up the ranks in the union, I think it bothers
him more and more. He's fiercely loyal to his union
and the men he represents. He'd rather do right by them
than negotiate or be conciliatory," she said evenly.

Her voice didn't reflect the turmoil that had arisen
unexpectedly upon seeing Kaliq. She had better get
used to it. She would be seeing a lot more of him when
they married.

His dark eyes had scarcely looked at her; he was
reading the union's list of demands. Demands beyond
the normal scope of their latest contract.

Now he glanced at her. "I asked Elise to find out
about getting married."

"I heard. I met half the office staff when I got off
the elevator. Our wedding is a seven-day wonder, and
curiosity is rampant."

"What?"

Molly smiled sweetly, though she longed to stamp
her foot. What had he been thinking? Probably hadn't
given the repercussions a thought. "News travels fast,
and everyone wants to know what we are doing. I understand we might even make a quick stop in Las Vegas for the ceremony."

He frowned. "I mentioned that in passing. I have no
intention of flying to Vegas. We can get married here
in New York. Elise will have all the information by
the time we're finished with LeBec. No one said anything to me."

"Like they're going to question the big boss?"

He stepped closer. "But they harassed you?"

"It's not harassment. Just friendly curiosity and open
season for gossip. The women here find you vastly ro-

mantic and think our marriage is a continuation of that romantic streak in you.''

At least she would be spared some of the speculation about her pregnancy when it became known—she hoped. She should be grateful for that. But she was still not feeling too charitable toward men. And it wasn't as if Kaliq wasn't getting what he wanted from the deal.

''Romantic? That's nonsense.''

''Oh, I don't know. I can see their point.''

He stepped closer. Molly felt the air leave the room. She would have moved back, gained some space, but she was already against her desk. If she didn't want to duck to one side like a gawky schoolgirl, she had to hold her ground. A deep breath—and she became conscious of Kaliq's unique scent, masculine and entirely too tantalizing. Molly longed for a moment's respite.

''You see their point? Maybe you could elaborate.'' His voice was low, husky. Instantly Molly imagined dark velvet-warm nights, Kaliq with a woman alone in a quiet place, talking, touching…

Her imagination soared out of control. Swallowing, she tried to find the words to make the man step back. But nothing came to mind except how she'd like to feel his lips on her own.

Why did she keep thinking about a possible kiss? She'd sworn off men!

''Molly?''

She cleared her throat. ''You are, um, rather, ah, exotic?''

''Exotic?''

''In a thrilling sort of way,'' she added rapidly, totally confused by the emotions that clamored within.

Was this some kind of hormone-induced fantasy? Was she losing her mind?

"Thrilling? You intrigue me. Please continue."

Oh, God, how did she get into this? Where was Frank LeBec? Wasn't he supposed to be here by now?

"Well, you're wildly attractive, tall, dark and handsome. Women notice things like that. And you're successful and rich and sophisticated and..."

He leaned even closer until Molly could feel the puff of his breath caress her cheeks. Mesmerized by his dark eyes, she couldn't continue. Could scarcely put two thoughts together. Her entire body seemed to be tuned to his, yearned for his, wished to explore that mouth that was so temptingly near. She longed to brush her fingers through that dark hair; test the strength of his muscles. Feel his heat envelop her.

"I'm fascinated by this discussion. Please continue," he said. His voice was like mulled wine—spicy and hot and intoxicating. Molly wanted him to speak, not her—so she could listen to his voice and float away on the myriad feelings that tumbled inside.

She leaned back over her desk, trying for some distance, some perspective. "Kaliq, you're crowding me."

"You've intrigued me, Molly. I'm interested to see if you feel as these other women do. If you find me exotic, fascinating, attractive."

His mouth was mere inches from hers. Molly wondered what he'd do if she just leaned forward until her lips touched his. Before she could gather enough wits to respond, however, he straightened and stepped back.

"Much as I'd like to continue this right now, I hear Elise approaching. Frank LeBec must be here." He moved to the door.

Molly remained rooted to the spot. If she didn't have the support of the desk behind her, she would have sunk to the floor. Taking a deep breath, she desperately sought control. She had a meeting to attend. No time to get starry-eyed about her boss or start imagining an attraction that wasn't there.

If his presence at work drove her wild, what would being married do? She had to keep control. She dared not imagine there was more to this relationship than was actually between them. She'd set herself up for heartbreak once. "Forewarned is forearmed," she muttered as she turned to get her notebook and a couple of pens.

Chapter Three

Molly knew she'd never make it through the day without going crazy. The meeting with Frank LeBec ended on a low note, from her point of view. She had not been so inattentive in a meeting since she'd first started and been scared to death she would do something wrong.

Yet how could she focus on business when her thoughts spun around her forthcoming marriage to Kaliq?

Would they find common interests or live parallel but separate lives? Did he plan to remain in the States his entire life, or did he expect to return to his own country at some point in the future when he turned over the reins of the shipping line to a younger family member?

And always at the back of her mind hovered the question of what he expected from their marriage.

What did *she* expect?

At the conclusion of the meeting, she had to run the

gauntlet through the office. Flustered by the time she reached her desk, she vowed next time she'd wait and walk with Kaliq. No one approached *him* with questions on how he saw their future.

Hoping to have a chance for a quiet lunch, she ordered from a nearby deli. She knew it reflected cowardice, but it also meant she could avoid her inquisitive co-workers for a while. If she stayed late tonight, she could avoid them all together.

Molly had just finished the last of her sandwich when Kaliq walked calmly into her office. He eyed the deli wrapping paper with distaste.

"If you are free for dinner this evening, shall we have it at my home? It will give you an opportunity to see the place and provide us with the time to speak privately about our plans."

Molly nodded, wadding up the wrapping paper and tossing it into the trash. "I could do that. You'll have to give me directions." She knew his apartment was on the west side of Central Park, but didn't know exactly where.

"No need, you'll be with me. Elise has found out what we need to do to procure a license. We'll leave this afternoon in time to arrive at City Hall before they close. Once we have the license, we must wait a day before the ceremony can be performed. Wednesday afternoon has been cleared. We'll be married then. Elise also located a moving company, which will pick up your furniture on Friday. If you'd prefer to be home on Friday when they arrive, we can work around that. Or I can have Hasim handle it."

"What?" Molly stared at him.

"Did you not hear me?"

Molly stood, unable to decide if she should laugh or

shout. A hint of temper simmered. She leaned over her desk slightly, eyes narrowed.

"Let me understand this, Kaliq. You've single-handedly arranged our entire wedding without consulting me? Arranged to move my stuff without even asking what I want to do?"

He nodded. "You were busy this morning. I need you to work on these negotiations, not become side-tracked with plans someone else can handle. I dele-gated the tasks to Elise, and she finalized them."

"So we marry on Wednesday. Did it ever occur to you that I might wish to have some friends attend my nuptials? Or that maybe I have something already planned for Wednesday afternoon?" Her voice rose on the last part and Molly took a deep breath.

It was nerves, nothing more. But the man was so arrogant sometimes she could hardly stand it.

"Do you?" he asked calmly.

Tilting her chin, she met his gaze. "What time? I'll check my calendar."

"Don't be foolish, Molly. I already had Elise verify that you'd be free. We agreed to marry as quickly as possible. Wednesday is not a busy day. Elise has can-celed all appointments except those directly involved with the negotiations. When would be a better time?"

"That's not the point."

"Ah, maybe I'm missing something in this discus-sion."

His use of the word "discussion" reminded her of their earlier "discussion." For a moment Molly was sidetracked as she remembered she'd thought he'd kiss her. But she quickly recovered.

"I need to get something to wear," she said, stalling.

He looked at the royal-blue silk blouse she wore with

a midcalf-length black skirt. "What you have on is lovely."

"Kaliq, I am not getting married in black!"

"Ah, I see there are subtle nuances to this marriage business."

She eyed his suspiciously. Was he mocking her? His bland expression gave nothing away. He'd been married before; he knew what was involved.

She wouldn't wear white, not four months' pregnant. But a nice cream-colored suit would work. If she could find one.

"In America, brides do not get married wearing black," she said.

"Nor do they in my country."

Molly hesitated. "I know very little about Manasia. Is it lovely? Or all desert?"

He laughed softly, his teeth startling white against his tanned face. "It is quite lovely, Molly. And a great deal is desert. But my family's home is on the edge of the Mediterranean Sea. The tangy scent of salt water mingles with the fragrance of jasmine when we are in the garden. It is wonderful to walk along the shore in the moonlight. It is not desert there. Away from the sea the land quickly becomes arid. Yet it holds its own beauty. I love to go riding across the vast expanse of open land that marks the southern boundary of my country. It is hot during the day, but cools off at night. When I can, I sleep in a tent with the Bedouins, eat dates and figs and exchange tales of long ago."

Excitement filled Molly as she listened to Kaliq describe his home. His voice took on a lyrical quality as he painted word pictures. She wistfully wished she could see it, experience it. It sounded romantic and mystical. Very unlike Ohio, and totally unlike New York.

"We must leave by four to accomplish everything. Tonight you will tell me of your parents and your childhood home. You have never mentioned them before," Kaliq said in a brusque tone.

"Of course not. Before this we had a working relationship. I don't mix work with personal."

"Indeed, you are a very private person, Molly. I look forward to learning many things about you in the weeks to come."

"I could say the same thing, Kaliq. I imagine I'll be pretty easy to know, but I'm not so sure about you."

Kaliq studied her thoughtfully for a moment, then turned to enter his office. Molly was quite unlike Sabrina. His personal assistant seemed almost fragile in comparison. His first wife had been wild and beautiful, demanding and restless. She had delighted in spending his money, buying clothes and furnishings and jewels like a child let loose in a candy shop.

He hadn't minded indulging her at first. It was only when he saw her true nature that he grew resentful of her love for his money. When he'd discovered she did not care for him as much as for his assets, and one of his business rivals, he'd started divorce proceedings.

He'd known Molly for five years—yet knew nothing beyond what she allowed. But he detected no wild extravagances in her life.

He wondered what the full story was with the man who'd fathered her baby. What was the private Molly like? Had she been devastated when the truth became known? For a moment he wondered if she'd have continued the relationship had there not been a baby.

No, not once she'd discovered the man was married. She was nothing like Sabrina.

In more ways than one. He remembered the jeans and the snug-fitting top she'd worn on Saturday. His first wife would not have been caught dead in such an outfit. Smiling slightly, Kaliq knew he couldn't wait to see Molly wear it again.

Crossing to his wide window, he gazed out over the busy city street without seeing a thing. He had wanted to kiss her that morning. The softness of her lips beguiled him, the warmth and suspected sweetness of her mouth tantalized. As did the feelings that still gripped him.

He had proposed this union to satisfy the INS. Now it looked as if he might get more from it than he expected.

Would Molly have kissed him back? Would she in the future? How far did they dare take this marriage and be able to break apart in a few months? Would she come to his bed?

Did he want her there?

He needed to understand her better before pushing for more. But with the sanctity of marriage between them, she couldn't refuse. They could enjoy each other, with no expectations to come crashing down later.

Except for the baby. What did he know about babies? They were innocent creatures, not deserving of some of the things fate had in store for them. He would not make the child his heir, and was pleased Molly had not expected it. Still, he could make sure it had a good start in the world.

For a moment he wondered if it would be a girl or boy. Would the child look like Molly? He could see a little chubby toddler with Molly's chestnut hair and wide gray eyes running around. Where would he be when the baby was two? Would they continue their arranged marriage or have long since parted?

"Are you ready?" Elise asked when she rang shortly before four o'clock.

"As I'll ever be," Molly replied. Quickly she straightened her desk, locking the sensitive folders in her drawer and stacking the rest of the papers. She slipped out to the ladies' room for a moment.

Checking to make sure her hair was neat, she studied herself in the mirror. She didn't look at all ruffled, yet inside, her stomach churned. She couldn't believe she'd agreed to this marriage. Was she crazy?

She took a deep breath and raised her chin. For better or worse, she was committed. It was just temporary. A solution to both their problems.

Kaliq waited for her in her office. He let his gaze run across her lightly, then took her arm. "Ready?" he asked.

"Yes." Molly felt his touch tingling in every cell. She had difficulty remembering he was her boss. Her clamoring senses wanted to deny that relationship and seek another.

Instantly the memory of his lips against her skin flashed into mind. Her wrist felt warm where he'd touched her. Licking her lips, she slid a glance sideways, almost feeling that kiss against her wrist. Would he kiss her on the mouth next time?

Her heart skipped a beat. She wasn't sure she could handle Kaliq. Yet the vague yearnings around him didn't make sense. Would she prove a satisfactory wife for him even temporarily? Or would he grow to regret his rash impulse before the situation was resolved?

"Kaliq?" she said when they were in the elevator. Amazing—they were alone.

"Yes?"

"If this doesn't work—"

"Why wouldn't it work?" he interrupted.

"I don't know, but I'm not sure I can pull it off."

"Pull what off?"

"Act like a wife for you."

"Let me be the judge of that, Molly."

The car stopped at another floor and three men entered.

Unwilling to pursue the conversation with others eavesdropping, Molly fell silent.

Kaliq flagged a cab with ease, handing her in and then climbing in beside her. Molly moved closer to the far door, but Kaliq's legs sprawled in the space, his knee touching hers. It was as if there was a direct link between them. Staring out the window, Molly saw nothing. Her entire body was focused on Kaliq and that spot where they touched.

It was distracting. She should be thinking about their marriage, making sure she knew what she was doing. Instead, she could only fixate on that connection with Kaliq and the roiling sensations that swamped her.

The cab ride to City Hall took longer than expected. Or had it only seemed endless? Molly wasn't sure.

In contrast to the ride, obtaining the marriage license seemed to take only seconds. And they were soon back in another cab and headed for Kaliq's apartment.

Molly was curious to see it. She wondered if there'd be room for any of her furniture. Would it blend in with his? Did he have very modern pieces and art she'd never understand?

He certainly was unlikely to have Early American

furnishings, which she loved. Maybe she'd just put her
things in storage for a few months. Or maybe leave
them where they were. She could continue to pay her
portion of the rent and move back in with Susan after
the marriage ended.

When the cab stopped before the tall stone building,
Molly realized the building sat directly across from
Central Park. Did his apartment overlook the park?
How nice to be so close to green space. Molly's spirits
rose.

"Remember, Molly, you may change things as you
see fit. This will be your home," Kaliq said as they
ascended in the quiet elevator. The lobby had been
small, but elegantly appointed. Kaliq had introduced
her to the doorman, telling him of their planned wedding and Molly's forthcoming move into the building.

Molly felt as if she had stepped into a dream.

The soft chime of the elevator and the doors sliding
open brought her back to reality. Kaliq used a key and
opened the door to his apartment, standing aside for
her to enter.

Stepping inside, Molly paused for a moment to take
in the surroundings. They had stepped into a small
foyer, with a long hall branching off to the left and
right. Moving farther into the apartment, she entered
the spacious living room. The wall opposite seemed to
be made entirely of glass. It overlooked the park. For
a moment she felt as if the room opened out and became a part of the outdoors. There were no curtains
cutting into the view, no shades to block the light. Just
a wide expanse of glass to admit the beauty of the park.

"Kaliq, this is wonderful!"

The room itself reminded her of the fantasy of the
Arabian Nights. Richly colored, thick Persian carpets

covered the floor. Her heels sank into them. Without thinking, Molly slipped out of her shoes and felt the lush carpets beneath her feet.

The furnishings defied categorizing. Low divans and plump cushions offered places to sit and recline. Equally low tables held plants or small bouquets of colorful flowers. Ancient tapestries depicting sweeping desert scenes hung on one wall.

The room felt spacious, open and untamed.

Her expectation of sophistication evaporated. This was unlike anything she could have imagined. And she loved it!

"I'm pleased you like it, Molly," Kaliq said quietly, studying her as she absorbed the beauty of her surroundings.

She turned to discover he was standing beside her, his head inclined as he looked into her eyes.

"If you wish to change anything, you may," he said.

"I don't think I'd want to. It's totally unexpected, but fantastic."

Her toes curled into the carpet as she tried to think of something else to say. To think up a reason to step away from the spell that held her captive. Kaliq stood so close she could reach out and touch him without moving but a few inches. His dark eyes seemed to look right down into her soul.

Shyly she smiled. "It reminds me of the *Arabian Nights*."

He nodded and she felt her heart skip another beat.

"I wanted the feel of the desert. When I visit home I often stay in tents furnished very like this. It must look odd to a Westerner—no draperies on the windows, no conventional chairs."

"It's different, but nice. I feel almost like I'm not in a room but a part of the outdoors. I like it."

Warmth filled her at his look. She felt almost light-headed.

The back of his fingers caressed her cheek, his fingers stopping beneath her chin, tilting her head to better gaze into her eyes.

"Good. Sabrina had the room entirely filled with modern furniture and dozens of knickknacks. It was too much. I find simplicity soothing, and beauty in the handiwork of God."

"At night what do you see?"

"We are high enough to be assured privacy. The sparkling lights from the buildings in the distance are enchanting. You will love it at night, as well. Ah, Hasim."

Kaliq lowered his hand and turned to greet the man who had silently stepped through the doorway.

"Molly, this is Hasim. Hasim, your new mistress, Molly Larkin, soon to be my wife. She and I will be married on Wednesday and she will move in immediately."

"Welcome, madam." Hasim was a tall man, dressed in a traditional dishdasha, the floor-length shirtdress of the desert. His head scarf was a red-and-white check. Because of his dress, he looked much more foreign to Molly's eyes than Kaliq, yet there was a similarity between the men. Both were tall, tanned from the hot sun of the Mediterranean, and spoke with slight accents. Kaliq had a British intonation. Hasim's was different.

Kaliq had been educated in England. Had Hasim learned English in Manasia?

"For the first few days things will continue as always, Hasim," Kaliq instructed. "After Molly's lived

here awhile, she may wish to make changes. You will
be guided by her decisions.''

"As you say." Hasim nodded his head once to Kaliq
and once to Molly.

"We'll have dinner at seven," Kaliq said.

Hasim nodded once more and quietly left the room.

"Come, I shall show you around the place," Kaliq
said, taking Molly's arm in a gentle clasp.

The familiar sensations began spiraling through her
body at his touch. She didn't understand it. She'd never
felt this way around Chad or any other man.

Gratitude, that was it. Kaliq was helping her beyond
what she should have expected. It was no wonder she
felt grateful to him.

By the time dinner was served, Molly's head was
spinning. The apartment consisted of twelve rooms.
Kaliq had shown her several bedrooms with en suite
baths, a study and a formal dining room, in addition to
a huge kitchen. Other than the spacious living room,
the rest of the apartment was furnished with more traditional Western furnishings—French provincial in one
bedroom, modern chrome and glass in another and
heavy Mediterranean in a third.

Kaliq's bedroom looked very ordinary, which surprised Molly. She wasn't sure what she'd expected—
more cushions on the floor or even a tent—but it wasn't
a king-size bed with a rather plain oak headboard, a
dresser and nightstand. Somehow his room should have
reflected the Arabian setting as did the living room.

"This will be yours," Kaliq said, opening an adjoining door. The room was tastefully decorated in soft
sea-green and bright yellow. "You may wish to have
your own furnishings in here. If so, Hasim can take
care of removing this furniture."

"This will be fine. Actually I thought I might just leave my furniture in my apartment. Then when we end the marriage, I can move back with minimum effort."

"Impossible, Molly. I thought you understood we must make certain we provide an impression to the INS of being completely committed. No one must suspect the reasons for this marriage, nor that we do not plan to remain together forever. You need to move in here. We will be a married couple sharing our lives."

"Oh, of course. I guess I didn't think it through," she murmured, annoyed with herself that she hadn't. The INS would be looking into all aspects of their marriage with a fine-tooth comb. And her keeping her apartment would be a blatant clue that all was not as it appeared.

"We will share the bath between the two rooms, if that is acceptable?" Kaliq asked.

"That will be fine."

And the INS also explained the reason for adjoining rooms. They had to look married—always. For a moment she wondered if she could go through with the charade, after all.

Kaliq looked at her sharply. "Something wrong?"

"No, not at all."

She couldn't meet his eyes. Instead, Molly studied the room as if her life depended upon being able to reconstruct it from memory. It was only for a few months. And she had her baby to think about.

"Molly—" Kaliq turned her to face him, his hands on her arms "—we have five bedrooms in this apartment. If this one doesn't suit, we can find another."

Yours?

Molly blinked and desperately prayed she had not

uttered the word aloud. Where had that thought come from?

She stepped back.

"No, really, Kaliq, this is perfect. And we need to keep up the pretense of a normal marriage."

"Unless such a time arrives that you feel comfortable sharing my room, perhaps?"

He did read minds! Mesmerized, she stood still, her eyes caught in his dark gaze, her tongue totally unable to form a single sound. Share Kaliq's room? His bed? Her heart thundered in response to the images that danced in her imagination. Of his strong sleek body pressed against hers, of his mouth kissing her as she had imagined only that morning. Escalating the spark of interest deep within until it raged as full-fledged desire. A conflagration only his touch could ignite, and extinguish.

"You never thought of that?"

His voice splashed through her like mulled wine, intoxicating every sense with its melodious tone. His head blotted out the rest of the room when he brushed her lips with his. Molly opened her mouth slightly and caught her breath.

"I'm not sure this is such a good idea," she whispered. Her voice wouldn't obey her. She wanted to sound firm and assured; instead she sounded breathless and uncertain.

"Ah, but we need to get to know each other better, right?" he said, his lips scant millimeters from hers. He closed the distance and kissed her long and deeply.

Molly felt as if she were floating, as the room spun round and round. The only solid anchor in a world turned topsy-turvy was Kaliq. Naturally she clung to that anchor. Her hands gripped his shoulders and she tilted her head slightly. Opening her mouth at his insistence, she felt the wonder of his kiss to her toes. Lost in the magic of his touch, she gave herself up to the sheer pleasure found in his arms.

When he pulled back, she was stunned at her reaction. There was no place for such activity in a business arrangement, and the sooner she made her position clear, the better. It was as if cold water had been dashed in her face. She stepped back, feeling almost bereft, but determined not to give in to temptation so easily in the future.

Was Kaliq assessing how willing a bride he'd acquired? Had the kiss meant anything to him?

Feeling lost, Molly brushed her hands down her skirt and turned to head back to the living room. Theirs was not a love match—she knew that better than anyone. And she didn't wish it to be. She'd experienced enough heartache and disappointment. She had no intentions of going down that path again!

Kaliq had proposed a business alliance and that was what she'd agreed to. His kisses were extraordinary. But she'd remain aloof, untouched. She didn't trust him, nor any man.

But the blood still raced through her veins, and her heart still beat heavily from the excitement of his embrace. She could tell herself to ignore him all she wanted, but she wondered if her body would ever listen.

"Come, we will sit in the living room and talk until dinner," Kaliq said.

Glancing at him as she passed, she was peeved to note he appeared totally unaffected by their kiss. Good! At least she tried to tell herself that.

* * *

Hasim had set the dinner table with beautiful china, elegant silver and delicate crystal, Molly noted when called to dinner some time later. The table looked fit for royalty. Which her future husband was in his country, she realized suddenly as she gazed at the dining-room table. Another problem?

Molly sat at Kaliq's right, doubts and uncertainty plaguing her.

"Do you dine like this every night?" she asked.

"No. Hasim has outdone himself tonight for the special occasion of your first meal with us."

"It's lovely. I wasn't sure if I had to live up to this on a daily basis." She should say something about the kiss, explain what she was willing to do for this marriage and what she was not willing to do, but the words wouldn't come.

"We will have a table like this for special events or when we have guests to dine."

"Otherwise it's paper plates in the kitchen, huh?" she said, trying to lighten the atmosphere.

His gleam of amusement brought a strong sense of satisfaction to Molly. Sometimes she wondered if she'd lose sight of who she was when she was with this man. Time to reassert her own personality. If he planned to go through with this charade, it was time he knew what he was getting.

Hasim entered, placing a bowl of soup before each of them.

"Perhaps not quite so casual. But the dishes we will normally use are not fine china. Do you like to cook, Molly? Will you be vying for time in the kitchen with Hasim?"

"No worry there. I like to bake brownies or cookies

once in a while, but I haven't done much cooking lately. It's hardly worth it for a single person.''

"Ah, but what about friends? Do you entertain?"

"Rarely. We usually go out and each pay our own way. After working all day, the last thing I want to do is more work, and that's what I think cooking is. Though my mother was a great cook.''

"Was she? Tell me about your parents, Molly.''

"My mom died when I was fourteen. My dad only a few weeks later. At the time, I thought he died of a broken heart. They were very close. I lived with an aunt until I moved here. Aunt Bea died just before I came to work for you. No other close family. Until my baby's born,'' she said briefly.

As the meal progressed, Molly found herself relaxing. The food was delicious, and American—prime rib, twice-baked potatoes and a collection of steamed vegetables. Another case of Hasim's outdoing himself for her first dinner? She didn't question it, just enjoyed every morsel.

"We'll take our coffee in the living room,'' Kaliq said at the end of the meal.

"Thank you, Hasim, it was perfect!'' Molly said as she rose to join Kaliq. "I'll skip the coffee, however. I'm not having caffeine these days.''

"My pleasure, madam,'' Hasim said formally.

"You've made his day,'' Kaliq said a few minutes later as they sat on the low divan in the living room. Hasim entered and set a tray before them on the low table, fragrant coffee in a fragile pot. A second pot contained hot water. Two cups and a small plate of assorted tea bags completed the tray. "Sabrina never said thank you or told him that a meal was delicious.''

"Hasim was here then?'' Molly asked as she poured

a cup for Kaliq, touched he'd also brought her tea. Did that show he approved of the forthcoming alliance? Or only that his training was excellent?

"Yes."

His clipped tone clued her in. He didn't want to discuss his ex-wife. Then why had he brought up her name?

"Shall we discuss the wedding?" she asked.

"It will be just the two of us and witnesses. Elise has scheduled it with a judge. Tomorrow you can find a suitable dress."

"So will we leave work early or just dash out on our lunch break?" She couldn't help the hint of impatience in her tone. Wasn't the bride supposed to have some say in her own wedding—no matter how arranged it was?

He glanced at her, raising one eyebrow. "We will be married at one, eat a celebration luncheon and then return home."

"Here, you mean?"

"Of course. This is your home now, Molly."

She didn't feel at home. Time would change that. At least she hoped so. Would it also change how she felt about Kaliq?

Exactly how did she feel about this man? Grateful he was willing to marry her. Intrigued by the personal glimpses she'd seen today. Fascinated by the attraction that seemed to grow every moment she spent with him.

But she would not forget for an instant that this was a temporary arrangement. No more fairy-tale love stories for her. Once they separated, she'd be free to live her life just as she wished.

For an instant Molly wondered if that would be enough.

Chapter Four

Tuesday Molly found it hard to concentrate at work. She arrived early to avoid other employees, asking Elise to run interference. Try as she might, she couldn't concentrate on the task at hand, but instead, kept remembering the previous evening with Kaliq.

Remembering and anticipating the next time the two of them were alone. Would he kiss her again? Touch her hand, brush back her hair? Looking up, she wished she could see behind closed doors.

When he'd arrived that morning, he'd gone straight to his office after a brusque hello and closed the door. She hadn't seen or heard from him since.

By noon Molly gave in. She couldn't do her job effectively. Instead, she'd go look for something to wear to her wedding.

Slipping past Elise, she told her she was taking the rest of the day off.

"Kaliq didn't mention that to me," Elise replied, checking her calendar.

"Yes, well he should have. If he asks for me, tell him I'll see him tomorrow."

"At the wedding. I'm attending, as well," the older woman said, her face wreathed in smiles.

"Good, I'll need all the friends there I can get." Oops, that didn't sound like a blushing bride. Pretense was harder than she suspected.

Elise looked startled. "Why?"

With another look at Kaliq's closed door, Molly sighed, trying to come up with a reason for her comment that would satisfy Elise.

"You know how forceful he can be. It's hard to hold my own sometimes." Like with the wedding arrangements that he'd made without a by-your-leave. Eyes narrowed, she glared at his door. Their marriage was for mutual convenience. She was bringing him something he couldn't get on his own, just as he was helping her out of a very awkward situation.

"I think being swept off my feet by such a handsome man would be thrilling," Elise said softly.

Molly turned her gaze to the older woman and noted the dreamy expression. Even Elise felt the magnetism. How was she supposed to resist if she was living with the man? Remembering the charade, Molly forced a smile.

"It is thrilling. He's wonderful. I think I just have prewedding jitters."

"Common, don't worry, they'll pass. When Joe and I married, I was a nervous wreck for weeks before the event. We had a big church wedding and—"

Elise stopped abruptly. "I guess it was different for us."

Molly nodded. "This will suit us both fine. I don't have any family, and my friend Susan will stand up with me tomorrow. I thought about inviting a few other friends, but decided we can have a reception later and invite everyone.'' Or not, since the marriage probably wouldn't last long enough to bother with such festivities. But no need to tell Elise.

"Anyway," Molly continued, "if he asks, tell him I've gone to get my wedding dress."

She stopped first for a quick bite to eat, then caught a cab to one of Manhattan's trendiest boutiques. She'd heard of the place for years and never considered entering it, much less buying something from it. But if her only wedding wasn't a time to splurge, Molly didn't know what would be.

The boutique was spacious and quiet, despite the numerous women shopping. A smartly tailored young woman came up to her only seconds after she entered. Within an hour Molly had the perfect silk suit and darling veiled hat. Matching accessories took only a bit longer, and by late afternoon she was on her way home. Extremely pleased with her selection, she hoped Kaliq would appreciate how nice she looked.

Susan was still at work and Molly had the apartment to herself. Changing into jeans, she began to sort and pack some of the things she'd take to Kaliq's apartment. Marking those items she wanted, she wondered if Susan would want the things she didn't care to move.

The phone rang.

"Hello?"

"Are you all right?" Kaliq's strong voice came across clearly.

"Sure. Why?"

"Elise said you left before lunch."

"And did she tell you why?"

He paused a moment. "No."

"Did you give her a chance to?"

"I called to get you, and when you didn't answer your phone, I called her. She said you'd left for the day, so I flicked it off and tried to reach you at home. There was no answer."

"I went shopping."

The silence stretched out for several seconds. "Shopping?"

"For a wedding dress. Remember, according to your very complete plan, Tuesday was the day to shop for a wedding dress."

"Ah yes, because black wouldn't suit."

"Right."

"So did you get one?"

"Yes, and it's definitely not black."

"White?"

"Sort of off-white. And a little hat with a veil." Did he care at all, or was she babbling to cover the nervousness that crept up? Sitting beside the phone, Molly took a deep breath. This was just Kaliq, her boss of five years.

And the man who had kissed her last night. A kiss like none other.

"So you will be the epitome of a traditional American bride."

"Maybe not the epitome, but fairly traditional. Is that a problem?"

"Not at all, I look forward to seeing you in the morning. Are you coming into the office first? Or shall I pick you up at noon?"

"I'm not coming to work at all tomorrow. Are you? It's our wedding day. And I certainly can't wear this suit to work. Besides, you can't pick me up. It's bad luck to see the bride before the ceremony. Susan and I will get a cab and meet you at the judge's chambers.''

"I'll send Hasim. He can drive you. And you can give him your bags. He'll bring them back to the apartment so they'll be waiting for you here when we return. I've had Elise book us for lunch at the Waldorf. I'll make sure she includes Susan.''

"Who else is coming?'' Molly asked, again a bit annoyed that he was arranging things without asking her opinion. Strong-willed and forceful he might be, but she was not going to let everything go his way.

"Elise, Phil Mannering and Abe Miller.'' Although Molly had never met Abe, she knew he and Kaliq had known each other for many years.

"Not your cousin Roeuk?''

The pause was barely discernable. "I have not yet informed my family of our marriage.''

"I see.'' But she didn't. Was it some big dark secret? Was he hoping to marry, get his green card and discard his new wife before his family learned of their nuptials?

"I doubt it, but I don't have time to go into that now. I'll see you tomorrow.''

"Kaliq, what did you want? Why were you trying to get me at the office?''

"I wanted the updated numbers on that new freighter in the Pacific, the *Alabaster*.''

"Those figures are in the left drawer, about three folders down. Elise can get them for you.''

"I'm not so helpless I can't get them myself,'' he returned dryly.

Kaliq hung up the phone thoughtfully. He had used that as an excuse to call her. When he'd discovered she'd left for the day, he'd immediately wondered if something was wrong. He didn't know much about pregnant women, only that they could suffer from morning sickness and other problems.

And for a split second he wondered if she was having regrets about agreeing to their upcoming marriage. Her buying the dress should reassure him. But it didn't.

He leaned back in his chair and turned to gaze out over Manhattan. It was unlike him to worry about what others did or thought. He'd moved beyond that a long time ago. He considered the solution he'd proposed perfect for them both. He'd keep his personal assistant and render her the help she needed. And he'd get his visa extended—permanently.

But was there more?

For a moment he let himself recall the kiss they'd shared last night. Molly had been sweet, shy and surprised. He felt it all. She could keep an impassive demeanor while working, but her emotions were clear to him last night.

And the pull of attraction surprised him.

He had dated before and after his brief marriage. Beautiful women, sophisticated, talented, articulate. Some he desired, many he did not. But none touched his sense of protectiveness like Molly. None raised questions that could only be answered by getting to know her better. Like he felt with Molly.

For having worked with her for five years, he really knew only the most superficial information about his assistant. Soon to be his wife.

He looked forward to discovering more aspects of her as they lived together.

And maybe explore that strong attraction.

* * *

Hasim picked up Molly and Susan early and delivered them to the courthouse. As they walked into the marble-floored lobby, Molly felt almost sick. She knew it wasn't from the pregnancy, but sheer nerves. She had not slept well. Worry about the advisability of taking this step plagued her.

"You okay?" Susan asked. They had been roommates for the five years Molly had worked at ALK Shipping. Susan was short, a bit plump and the best friend Molly had ever had. "You look a bit green around the gills."

"Great, I hope the color goes well with my suit."

"You look fine, just a bit off color. Having doubts?" Susan was the only person besides Molly and Kaliq who knew the entire story behind the wedding. "It's not too late to say no."

"And do what—move to California?"

"I've told you a dozen times that no one pays that much attention to unmarried mothers these days."

"And I've told you back that it would matter to me. Blame it on my small-town upbringing. Anyway, I'm committed. Just a bit nervous."

They found the judge's chambers and entered. Kaliq was already there, standing near the window conversing with the judge, Phil and another man Molly didn't recognize. Must be his long-time associate, Abe. Did he ever think to call him a friend?

"Wow!" Susan said. "Is that hunk by the window the groom? Tall, dark and devilishly handsome? If you don't fall madly in love with him, send him my way!"

Molly swallowed. The last thing she wanted to do was fall in love with anyone! Much less Kaliq bin Shalik.

He looked up and saw her. Without a word to the

men he'd been talking with, he crossed the room to her.

"Molly." He reached for her hand and kissed the palm, enclosing it in his own as he turned to Susan.

"You must be Susan."

"Yes, Susan Abernathy. I guess you're Kaliq."

"I'm pleased Molly has a good friend to join us today."

"I just hope this all works."

He raised an eyebrow and looked at Molly.

"The marriage and all," she said. "Is everyone here? Are we ready to start?"

He pulled her slightly to one side and reached for a small florist box on the table.

"I took the chance the colors would suit," he said, offering her the box.

When Molly opened it, she found a lovely corsage of pink roses and white baby's breath. Susan stepped up and helped her fasten it to her suit.

"Now you really look like a bride," her friend said, giving her a hug.

Elise hurried in, and with the entire wedding party present, they were ready to start.

The judge began the familiar service and Molly listened as if in a trance. The opening was nice, and sounded just as if they were truly getting married. Which they were, she reminded herself. Just because it seemed like a dream didn't mean it wouldn't be legal and binding.

"Do you, Molly, take Kaliq to be your lawful wedded husband, to love, honor and obey, in sickness—"

Molly became instantly alert.

"Wait."

The judge stopped. Kaliq looked at her.

"Say that part again."

The judge began again and as soon as he reached the word *obey,* Molly stopped him.

"No." She turned to Kaliq. "No 'obey' in the vows. I never agreed to that. I'm not some child to be directed by someone else."

"Molly, it's just part of the ceremony."

"No."

With a suppressed sound of frustration, Kaliq took her arm and walked her across the room where they'd have a modicum of privacy.

"What's going on?" he asked, leaning close, his glare capturing Molly.

"I'm not going to promise to obey you unless you promise to obey me and say your part first. That's all. I didn't know he would use such an antiquated ceremony. I know the newer version doesn't say 'obey.'"

"For the love of Allah, Molly, it's just a ceremony."

"And can you promise me in all the time we'll be married you will never say to me you must do it my way or you must obey me in this because you promised when we were married?"

He stared at her for endless moments. "I would not say that."

"Ha! Kaliq, I've worked with you for five years. I know how you work. When you really want something, you go after it with everything you have. And this is just the perfect thing to add to your arsenal when making a point."

"I can't believe you've stopped everything over one word."

"Then eliminate the word or include it in your vows. Your choice."

He shook his head and looked around. The others

were waiting near the judge, watching them curiously. Susan fought a smile. Even Abe seemed amused.

Looking back at Molly, Kaliq asked softly, "Are you going to be this difficult all the time?"

She smiled at him and shook her head. "Consider this our first compromise. And isn't that a big part of marriage? Compromising so we both come out ahead?"

"It shall be as you wish." He inclined his head once and then started back toward the judge.

Molly didn't know if she could claim a victory or not. But at least she'd stood up for herself. She knew she had to make sure Kaliq didn't swamp her.

After a brief conference with the judge, Kaliq indicated he should continue, which he did—omitting "obey" from her vows.

"You may kiss the bride," the judge ended.

Kaliq brushed a light kiss across her lips and turned to shake the judge's hand.

Molly felt disappointed. She had expected more. For a moment she thought she might cry. Was that it? A light brush of lips for the wedding kiss? The kiss in the apartment the other night had held more emotion, more passion.

"Congratulations!" Susan hugged her.

Then Elise. Abe shook her hand, offering his best wishes.

"I brought a camera. Want some pictures with the judge?" Susan asked. "I'm your official wedding photographer."

"I brought my camera, as well," Elise added. "Wouldn't be a wedding without pictures."

Molly smiled, though she felt shaky and uncertain inside. Would Kaliq stand for further nonsense about a wedding, or now that the deed was done, would he hasten back to work after lunch to have the legal department contact the INS?

He surprised her. When Susan told him what she wanted, he posed with Molly, his arm around her waist, pulling her close to him. She could smell the scent of his aftershave, which brought memories of the night at his apartment.

The warmth of his hand against her waist spread. Her breathing caught and for a moment she felt lightheaded. Her blood pounded through her veins and echoed in her ears.

Smiling, turning this way and that, she made it through the battery of pictures both Susan and Elise insisted upon. But she felt disjointed, out of control. Kaliq bin Shalik was her husband. She was no longer Molly Larkin, but Molly bin Shalik, wife of an Arab Sheik!

Lunch was a blur. She hoped she talked coherently, but couldn't remember a single sentence.

Settled after lunch in the extravagant limousine Kaliq had hired, Molly suddenly longed for her freedom. She'd had it made when she was single. She could go where she wanted, do what she wanted.

Now she had agreed to a marriage to provide Kaliq a way to remain in the U.S. and save her own pride when the pregnancy became obvious. She had to play her part of loving devoted wife well to allay any suspicion of the INS—or the gossips at work.

Could she do that? Pretend to feel strongly for her husband while all the while trying to keep her distance? She couldn't let herself fall for him, as Susan had suggested. She already knew she wasn't his type. If a worldly beauty like Sabrina couldn't hold him, how could a woman from a small town in Ohio?

"Tired?" Kaliq asked as the limousine slid quietly through the Manhattan traffic.

"No. Still keyed up a bit."

"Despite your interruption, the ceremony went well. I liked it better than the elaborate affair Sabrina dreamed up."

Ignoring the reference to his first wife, Molly gazed out the window. They were heading uptown—toward his apartment. Their apartment.

"Are you planning to return to work today?" she asked.

"No. If we are fostering the impression this is a true marriage, I don't see a doting husband deserting his wife on their wedding day."

"I guess not."

"In fact, we are taking the rest of the week off."

She looked at him in surprise. "We are? Kaliq, you need to work on your husband skills. You don't just announce things. We need to discuss them and decide mutually what we'll do."

His eyes danced with amusement. "I see I have created a different person in Molly the wife from Molly the personal assistant."

"I start as I mean to go on," she said defensively.

"And for how long will we go on? I wonder," he said.

"What do you mean?"

"We agreed to marry for expediency. But I've been thinking that it might work out well enough to continue even after your baby is born and I have the green card. Unless, of course, you have other plans."

She shook her head. Had she heard him correctly?

He'd be interested in continuing this marriage of convenience indefinitely?

"Only time will tell, I think," he said.

Hasim greeted them when they arrived at the apartment.

"I've put your bags in your room, madam. If you wish for me to unpack, please tell me."

"No, that's all right, I can manage," Molly said quickly. She needed something to keep her busy for the afternoon.

"Change into something you find comfortable and join me in the living room when you feel like it," Kaliq suggested.

Molly took her time changing and sorting and putting away her clothes. The closet was huge and her few skirts, business suits and dresses looked lost. The built-in shelves would hold twice as many clothes as she had brought.

She gazed at the view from her window. If she angled her head just right, she could get a view of the park. But the living room was the place to be for that view.

Wishing she didn't feel awkward and uneasy, she finally decided she couldn't remain in her room forever.

Wandering into the living room, she was disappointed to find she was alone. She thought Kaliq would be impatiently waiting for her.

Hasim appeared as if summoned.

"Would you like something to drink, madam?"

"Do you have any fruit juice?" she asked.

"Certainly. We have orange, apple, cranberry and grape."

"That's quite a selection. I'll have some cranberry juice."

He inclined his head. "His Excellency said you were expecting a baby, so I made sure we have food and beverages that will be of healthy benefit."

Flustered, she nodded and watched as he almost glided from the room.

His Excellency. Kaliq. She knew he was Arab royalty, but with that one title, Hasim had clearly demonstrated to her just how far out of her league Kaliq really was.

Not that she expected anything to come of their hasty marriage. No matter what he said about seeing how long they might wish to continue their marriage, there were too many differences between them. The major one being status in life.

"I like that shirt." Kaliq stood in the opening from the hall.

Molly turned and stopped dead. Kaliq had donned loose-fitting flowing white trousers that probably came directly from the Arabian desert. His loose shirt reminded her of pirates, or desert sheiks of old who captured beautiful maidens and took them to their tents in the desert.

Tied loosely, the shirt exposed a wide V of his chest. Molly's eyes fastened on that bare strip of skin, and she couldn't look away.

He'd always looked wonderful in his tailored suits. Now he was breathtaking. Sexy and virile and almost overwhelmingly masculine.

Her fingertips itched to explore that broad chest, to touch his skin, feel the heat pour into her. Her heart sped up like she'd just run a race.

He came into the room as lithely as a panther, sleek and smooth. Her heart skipped a beat.

"Is Hasim taking care of you?"

"He's bringing me some juice." It was with monumental effort she raised her gaze to meet his eyes. Licking her suddenly dry lips, she cleared her throat.

"He knows I'm pregnant."

"I told him. Just, as I guess from her comment, you told your roommate the truth about our marriage."

"Susan won't tell anyone."

"And if Immigration asks her questions?"

"Why would they?"

"If they suspect this marriage is false, they may question everyone who knows us."

"She's starting her vacation this weekend. She's going to Mexico for an archaeological dig. By the time she gets back, the decision will surely have been made. She's my best friend. She would have suspected something was amiss when I went to work planning to give notice and returned engaged."

"Your powers of persuasion could not have convinced her you fell madly in love and agreed to my proposal for that purpose?"

She grinned. "Nope. My powers of persuasion are not *that* strong!"

"And there is the baby's father. Do you still love him? Miss him?"

Molly shrugged and turned away, strolling over to the wide expanse of windows.

"I don't think so. I'm more angry than anything when I think of him. If he truly loved me as he told me, why would he have let our relationship go so far without telling me the truth?"

"Perhaps he does love you and cannot get out of the

marriage. I can see a man wanting to keep you—no matter what the cost.''

Molly spun around—to find Kaliq right beside her. How had he crossed the room so silently? She turned the wedding band on her finger, uncertain how to take his comment.

''Why, Your Excellency, are you flirting with me?''

He went still. ''Your Excellency?''

''Isn't that the correct way to address you? Hasim said—''

''Ah, Hasim. We are in America now. You don't have royalty.''

''But in your country—''

''When we get to my country, we'll see how things work out. In the meantime, come and tell me something personal about my new wife.''

He led her to one of the low divans. Sinking on the cushions, Molly wondered how she'd ever get up again. But they felt wonderful. Looking out the window, she felt as if she were on top of the world.

''What do you want to know?'' she asked.

''What you were like at age five.''

''And if I tell you that, will you share with me?'' She would be fascinated to learn about his childhood. About life in his country. It sounded so faraway and so exotic.

''Of course, isn't that also a part of marriage—in addition to the compromises you spoke of?''

Hasim brought juice for them both and quietly retired.

Hesitating only a moment, Molly began to talk about her childhood in Elmsville, Ohio. Wondering how different it was from his, she told about her first bicycle, about starting school and about slumber parties.

She kept her gaze firmly fixed on the view of the park, and not on the sight of Kaliq sprawled so casually beside her on the wide divan, lest she become tongue-tied and forget what she wanted to say.

His hand unfastened her clip and combed through her hair.

She stopped talking and looked at him, her eyes wide with wonder.

"Your hair has sunshine in it," he said whimsically. "And it's as soft as the finest silk." His fingers toyed with strands, touching each as if memorizing the texture.

Leaning across her, he gathered it in both hands and brought it up near her face.

"I've seen it worn pulled back for five years. But never like this, soft and full around your face." He spoke as if talking to himself. "It suits you."

"It's easier to keep it pulled back at work," she said breathlessly.

"Ah, but more feminine like this."

Slowly he leaned forward and Molly held her breath.

Chapter Five

Molly's heart raced as she parted her lips. She knew she'd lost her mind. Instead of anticipating Kaliq's kiss, she should jump up and put the length of the room between them.

In a minute.

First she wanted—

Hasim cleared his throat.

Kaliq slowly released the cascading waves of hair and sat back, looking impassively at his servant.

"Yes?"

"Excuse the intrusion, Excellency. Mr. Mannering is calling. He says it's urgent." Hasim held out a cordless ivory phone.

Kaliq took it and sat up.

"Yes?"

Molly struggled to rise from the low divan. She ignored Hasim and walked to the floor-to-ceiling windows to gaze sightlessly out on the springtime beauty of Central Park. She hugged herself as she tried to find some rational thought. What was she doing letting herself be seduced by Kaliq? Hadn't she learned enough from her experience with Chad to know that men had their own agenda?

It was easy for Susan to fantasize about Kaliq; she didn't have to live with him or work with him. Or consider what their next step would be. Molly did.

She needed to be very careful not to let herself be caught up in the make-believe world they were creating. He valued her as an employee—this absurd idea of marriage proved that. Plus, she was in a position to help him out.

Nothing had changed. Unless he thought because they were married he could now change that relationship.

"Molly."

She turned. He'd laid the phone on the low table.

"What did Phil have to say?" she asked, keeping her distance. They had to settle things before she'd feel comfortable again.

"He contacted Immigration. They are naturally suspicious, considering the haste of our wedding. We are to meet with the inspector day after tomorrow. If he is not satisfied with our explanation, the deportation will go forward."

"Then we have to make sure he is satisfied, don't we?"

"A single interview with us will probably not be the end of it."

Molly shrugged. "We'll do the best we can."

"And as long as we present a united front to the world, he won't find anything amiss."

She eyed him suspiciously. "What does a 'united front' mean?"

Slowly he smiled. Molly felt her heart melt. Did he have a clue how devastating that smile was? How it made her feel tingly inside as if her blood were filled with effervescent bubbles like fine champagne?

"To the world we appear as a devoted couple. We'll start at the party Sven Johannsen is giving Friday night. He has a new artist as protégé and is hosting a showing at the gallery on Fifth Avenue."

"This Friday night?"

"Yes. I've already accepted the invitation. You'll attend with me, of course."

"You must have been sure you wouldn't be deported! Don't you think you could have asked me first?"

He rose with one easy move and walked across the room to her.

Or at least Molly tried to think of it as walking, though it had the earmarks of a panther stalking his prey. Controlled, smooth, but focused and direct.

She swallowed hard. *Start as you mean to go on,* she admonished herself.

"Listen, Kaliq, if this is going to work at all, we have to come to some kind of understanding. At work you're the boss. What you say goes. But this isn't work. If you want me to consider this my home, then I get some say in things."

He nodded once, his attention focused on her.

Molly took a deep breath. "If you want to do things as a couple, then I need to be given the chance to participate in making plans."

"These plans were made before we even discussed our marriage."

"Then I don't need to go. They obviously were satisfied with you coming alone before. Nothing has to change.''

''Don't be naive. Can you imagine the rampant rumors if I show up two days after the wedding without my wife? You're going!''

Holding on to her temper by a thread, Molly tried to find a way to make him understand. She'd had years of practice dealing with his high-handed way of working. Surely she could find a satisfactory way to have a harmonious home life for however long the marriage lasted.

''Maybe I have other plans. Maybe—''

''Cancel them,'' he said ruthlessly.

She blinked. ''Kaliq, this is not going to work if you think you can order me around! This isn't the army, and you're not my commanding officer!''

''Army? What are you talking about?''

''You! You are so used to ordering everything. But not in a relationship with a woman!''

''Do you have other plans?'' he asked ominously.

She shook her head. ''That's not the point. I might have. All I want is for you to see me as a person in my own right—to be asked.''

He took a deep breath, running the fingers of one hand through his hair. ''Molly, I have an invitation to a party at Sven Johannsen's on Friday night. Would you do me the honor of attending with me?''

She smiled and nodded. ''I would love to go.''

He frowned. ''Are you playing games?'' He stepped closer.

Bravely Molly held her ground.

''No, just establishing ground rules, I guess.''

''I don't remember having had a lot of complaints from other women I've taken out.''

"Then they spoiled you. You've lived in America long enough to know women like to be independent."

"I've had no complaints from you over the last five years."

"Kaliq, what I put up with at work isn't the same as what I'm willing to put up with at home!"

"Kal."

"What?"

"Call me Kal. It's the name my family and close associates use."

He reached out and brushed her hair back from one cheek, letting the back of his fingers caress her skin.

"Your skin is as soft as a baby's. And your hair is like hot silk."

"K-k-kal." She stopped, cleared her throat. "Kal, I don't think we should be doing this."

Where was the decisive tone she needed? Her voice came out breathless and faint.

"Ah, but don't you think a husband and wife are allowed a certain amount of, shall we say, intimacies?"

"But this is just pretend."

"The feelings I am experiencing right now don't feel like pretend."

Slowly he drew her closer.

Molly put up her hands to push him away. Only, when her fingers touched the heat of his skin, she lost the will to push. She wanted to explore, to touch him, to uncover every bit of the mystery surrounding her desert sheik.

When he kissed her, she forgot even that quest. Parting her lips, she returned his kiss with rising passion. Caught up in the moment, she could only hang on while her senses soared. She delighted in the feel of his hard body against hers, in the pleasure that cascaded through her.

When he ended the kiss, he didn't pull away, but trailed nibbles along her cheek, to her neck and throat, kissing the wild pulse point at its base.

Molly didn't know how her arms came to be holding him, or how her fingers became threaded through his thick hair, but she took advantage of the situation, exploring, exalting in the sensations that continued to sweep through her.

He wanted her. She was experienced enough to know that. For a moment she almost gave in to impulse.

But caution held her back. Had her slowly release her hold.

Kaliq must have felt the change, because the kisses became lighter, until they were no more.

He rested his forehead on hers and gazed into her eyes.

"We are married, Molly. And I have not lived like a monk. But we are not going to do anything to ruin this relationship. If you want to take it beyond the platonic, let me know. Otherwise…"

She nodded. She didn't know what she wanted. Right now she wanted to have more kisses, to feel his hands on her body, to know the soaring ecstasy she suspected only Kaliq could give her.

But she didn't trust herself with men anymore. How did she know what the real agenda might be? After Chad…

No, she was not there again. He was her past. Kal was her future.

But she was too unsure of anything right now to bank on that future.

Gently disengaging herself, she tried to smile. Knowing it was a futile effort, she stopped. "I guess we need to see how it goes before taking any steps that might complicate things."

He straightened to his full height and looked down at her.

"Especially when what I have to say will offer another complication."

"What?"

"I think until the INS has finished its investigation, you need to share my room."

Stunned, Molly widened her eyes. Had she heard him correctly?

"Share your room—your *bedroom?*"

"Phil went over some of the questions he suspects the investigator will ask. Like, have we consummated this marriage? Do we share a room? A bed? How long have we been in love? Did we date?"

Molly could not have said a word if her life depended on it. She was looking forward to the sanctity of her bedroom at night. A place where she could escape Kaliq's strong attraction and magnetism for a while each day.

Now he wanted to take that away? Have her share his room?

He smiled, though no amusement showed in his eyes. "Thanks. Your faith is overwhelming."

"I didn't say anything."

"Don't ever play poker, Molly. Your expression gives away everything."

"That's not true. I have a great poker face. Look at how I do at work."

"Trust me, I could tell you are not thrilled with this complication."

She took a deep breath. The day was taking on a surreal atmosphere. "What else? Might as well get everything out in the open. Any other 'complications'?"

"Would that be such a hardship? To sleep in my bed? It's quite large, and I don't move around a lot."

Sleep. A euphemism for making love. Not that Kaliq meant that. They'd just sleep in the same bed. That huge king-size bed she'd caught a glimpse of when touring the apartment.

"Okay. What else?"

"When around others, we need to act like we are a devoted couple."

"You said that before. What do you mean by 'devoted'?"

He encircled her neck with one hand and pulled her closer. "Touching, smiling into each other's eyes like we hold the secret of the universe." He demonstrated and Molly's knees went weak.

What would she give to have a man look at her like this and mean it? She'd always wanted to fall in love and get married. Instead, she'd fallen in love with the wrong man and married a different one.

One who could capitalize on her vulnerability right now and have her imagining she was falling in love with him!

"You're not doing your part. Is this another instance where I have to ask?" he said softly, cajolingly.

Slowly Molly relaxed. Gazing up into Kal's eyes, she let a hint of emotion creep into hers. Smiling as seductively as she could, she reached up and brushed his lips with her fingertips.

"I'll give it my best shot, darling," she said huskily.

He groaned and stepped back.

"It's easier to deal with women in my country than

contrary Americans," he said, turning. He walked to the table and reached for his glass, draining the juice.

Feeling she'd held her own, Molly didn't know how long she could hold out against the strong pull of attraction her new husband engendered.

The sooner they got things back to normal, the better.

As if Kal had heard her thoughts and agreed with them, he became the perfect host to a guest in his home. He showed Molly his stereo system and let her skim through the collection of CDs. She liked many of the musical groups he had acquired, and they played familiar tunes during the afternoon.

They changed for dinner, Molly wearing a black dress that showed off the gold jewelry she favored. Joining Kaliq in the dining room, she almost complimented him on the dark suit and white shirt he wore. Once again he was the man she'd worked with for five years.

Seeing that relaxed her. Things would work out. The wild Arabian prince of the afternoon was only one facet of her husband. This one she knew.

Hasim prepared a huge feast for a wedding celebration, complete with champagne. Molly took only a sip of hers to join in the mood. But when Kaliq seemed to enjoy his, she frowned.

"I didn't think you drank alcohol," she said.

"I don't imbibe often, and rarely at home. But my favorite aunt is from France. Her influence in our family is strong. From religion to education to knowledge of fine wines, she played a major part in our values. Roeuk's mother. You've met my cousin."

"Yes. There is a family resemblance."

"He has an American wife. I'll have to ask him for pointers."

She gave a mock frown. "A little consideration is all I'm asking."

He laughed and raised his flute. "May all our days be as delightful as this one has been, Molly."

Pleased with the toast, she touched her own glass to his and sipped.

Molly had not expected a honeymoon. But Kaliq had told her yesterday that he had planned for them both to take the rest of the week off from work. She was astonished when she rose the next morning to discover Kaliq had left for the office at his usual early hour.

"I am to give you this note," Hasim said when she asked after her husband. "It would be my honor to prepare you a Western breakfast. Would you like eggs?"

Molly opened the note and scanned the contents. Kal had gone in for a little while. If she awoke before he returned, he hoped she would make herself at home. And perhaps move her things into his room. Tonight they would share a bed to be able to answer the INS's questions with all the honesty possible.

And perhaps she wished to shop today for something to wear to the party. What was suitable for a personal assistant might not be suitable for his wife.

Molly crumpled the note into a ball. If he'd been near, she'd blister his ears with her thoughts about his suggestion.

"Madam?"

"I'll take a poached egg on dry toast and some herbal tea."

"There is an assortment already at the table. I'll bring you boiling water and prepare your breakfast."

Fuming, Molly followed Hasim into the dining room. How dare Kaliq suggest her clothes were not suitable! They were stylish and of good quality.

Suitable for the wife of a wealthy international businessman? a voice inside whispered.

She sat and picked a packet of tea. Fixing the hot brew, she considered her options. She could feed her anger and let loose when he returned. Or she could go buy the most expensive dress she could find and see how he liked that.

She didn't care that her reaction was childish; he made her so mad sometimes. It would serve him right if she sent him the bill.

He won't mind, that voice said.

Which was probably true. He had enough money to buy that boutique she'd tried with pocket change.

After dawdling over breakfast as long as she could, Molly gave up waiting for Kaliq. If he didn't want to give rise to speculation, why had he gone in to work as usual? She would not. This was her honeymoon, even though they were not going anywhere. She would put the time to good use.

Heading out, Molly made plans.

Her first stop was the boutique. Recklessly she told the saleswoman that she wanted the most outrageous dress they had. It would put a huge dint in her savings, but she didn't care.

Trying on dress after dress, none of them seemed just right. She wasn't sure what she was looking for— something to make a statement and drive the point home to her new husband.

When the salesclerk brought in a red dress, Molly

knew it was the one. Trying it on, she crossed her fingers it would still fit. She wasn't showing much in her pregnancy yet.

The dress slid over her like a second skin. It was one-shouldered, so that her left arm and shoulder were bare. It scarcely reached the top of her knees. Shimmering in the light, it was a sexy siren of a dress.

"Wow," she said.

"Wow is right," the saleswoman agreed. "If that doesn't get him to sit up and take notice, forget the man. He's dead."

Molly glanced at her. "You think this is for a man?"

"Why else?" the woman asked, amusement dancing in her eyes. "You want to try to tell me different?"

Molly laughed. "No. I'll take it. Shoes?"

"We have some strappy high-heeled sandals that would be perfect for that dress. Let me see if we have your size."

While she waited, Molly turned this way and that before the mirror. She looked totally different, wild and free. And as unlike Kaliq's staid personal assistant as it was possible to get.

Her heart sped up when she thought of Kaliq's reaction when he saw her.

Throwing caution to the wind was fun, she decided. As long as she could handle things. And she thought she could. Their understanding was firm. No falling in love on either side.

He'd been burned by Sabrina, and she by Chad. They had a mutually beneficial agreement that suited them both.

But if he planned to throw in complications like sharing a bed, she wasn't going to sit idly by.

"Try these." The saleswoman handed Molly the shoes.

They were perfect. Molly hummed happily as she changed back into her street clothes.

As the salesclerk wrapped the dress and shoes, she glanced at Molly hesitantly. "I'm stepping out of line with this, but I would suggest a new hairstyle. Something short and sassy that will complement the dress. Or have it done up in an elaborate cascade."

Molly nodded. It was worth thinking about.

Hadn't Kaliq just yesterday said he liked her hair around her face?

Not that she would change her hairstyle because of his comment. But another style would look better with the dress.

Molly hurried back to the apartment, placing her new dress in her closet. She spent part of the afternoon moving her other clothes to Kaliq's closet. And to the drawers Hasim had cleared for her.

Feeling odd at sharing the space, Molly left as soon as everything was put away.

Where was Kaliq?

She phoned the office and learned that he was tied up with LeBec.

It was late by the time Molly heard the door to the apartment open. She had given in to Hasim's entreaties and eaten hours earlier.

Kaliq appeared in the doorway, and Molly put down her book.

"Tough day?" she asked.

He looked tired around the eyes. She had never noticed that before. Was she growing more attuned to the man?

"More so than usual." He loosened his tie and shrugged out of his suit jacket.

"Go change, and I'll get Hasim to fix your dinner. I already ate."

"I hoped you would." He hesitated a minute, then nodded. "I won't be long. I didn't mean to desert you on our first day together. But the negotiations need to get out of the logjam or we'll be stalemated when the contract expires."

"I know that."

He nodded. "I missed my personal assistant today."

"Nice to be appreciated. Maybe I should hit you up for a raise next Monday."

"Maybe I'll give you one without being asked."

Molly smiled as she listened to him walk down the hallway. One more weekday to play honeymooner, then they'd be back at work on Monday and things would be as close to normal as they would get for the next few months.

Kaliq brought her up-to-date while eating dinner. She realized she had worried he would close her out of the loop once they married. But he didn't.

"Tomorrow morning we have the interview with the Immigration Department. And the party in the evening," Kaliq said.

"I have an appointment to have my hair done in the afternoon," she mentioned casually. Would he like her hair short? Or did he like it long? Doubts assailed her.

They were chased away when it came time to retire. Tonight Molly was sleeping in Kaliq's bed. With him. Tomorrow could take care of itself. She had tonight to worry about.

When he said he wanted to check his messages in his home office, Molly took the time to hurry to the bedroom. Clad in a full-length nightgown that tied at the neck and had long lacy sleeves, she slid into the bed and clung to the edge. She wasn't sure which side she should sleep on, but took a hint from the clock by the far side. Surely it was placed close by so he could silence the alarm each morning.

Despite the worry about the sleeping arrangement and tomorrow's pending meeting, Molly fell asleep long before Kaliq joined her.

The next morning the bed showed signs of his occupancy, but Kaliq was already up when she awoke.

Stretching, she reached out to touch the pillow he'd used. He had been right, darn him. Nothing had happened and the bed was plenty large enough for them both. She had never known he'd joined her last night.

Dressing, she hurried to the dining room. Kaliq had finished eating and was sipping coffee as he read the paper.

"Good morning. I hope I'm not late," Molly said as she took the chair to his right.

"We have plenty of time. Are you ready? Phil told me yesterday they would probably interrogate us separately."

"Oh. Okay, I guess. What are we saying?"

"We've worked together for five years. During that time we've grown close. Not realizing how close until it looked as if I was being deported. Then you confessed your love for me and I said—"

"Wait a minute. I confessed my love for you? Try it the other way around."

"Molly, now is not a time to be contrary."

"It works just as well the other way. You found out you were being deported and hated to go—not because of work, that would get done with your excellent managers—but because you'd have to leave me.'' She smiled brightly. "I really think that is much better.''

Kal frowned, but gave the matter serious consideration. "Maybe you're right. It takes the emphasis off the business.''

"I'll want a really large raise,'' she said smugly.

Three hours later Kaliq handed Molly into a cab and followed her. He settled back as the driver slid into the busy traffic.

She leaned closer to whisper in his ear. "I think we pulled it off, don't you? It went so smoothly!''

He nodded, his eyes on the cabdriver. The man ignored them as he fought the heavy midtown traffic.

Kaliq looked at Molly. She was glowing with happiness. There was more to go through, but she was right—it did look as if the inspector believed their story. Of course, bringing in her pregnancy helped. Kaliq knew the man thought the child was his.

For a moment he wondered what it would be like to be a father. To take turns rocking a cranky baby, to watch his wife nurse their child at her breast. To watch Molly shower her love on the baby.

Her scent reached him, light and fragrant. Lilacs, he thought. He was used to it, for she wore it all the time. Used to it, but attracted just the same.

Damn, he was finding that more and more. When had Molly changed from a perfect personal assistant to a woman who captured his attention?

She'd been giving and passionate in the kisses they'd shared. Yet last night, despite the warmth in the apartment, she had worn a virginal gown to bed that covered her from head to foot. At least, he imagined it was long.

She'd had a warm flush on her face when he finally joined her. He'd watched her sleep for several long moments, trying to figure out what had changed between them. And why he had this need to know about her, to touch her, feel the delicate texture of her skin.

Why he wanted to kiss her. Why he wanted her.

He looked out the window. Things had changed, but he had not. Hadn't Sabrina proved that women wanted what men could give them, but not the men themselves? In this, Molly was no different. She wanted the safety of marriage because of her unexpected pregnancy.

He better never forget that. No matter how much he wanted his wife.

"I've changed my mind, driver," Kaliq said, giving him the office address. To Molly he said only, "Since you'll be busy this afternoon, I might as well go in to the office for a few hours." To escape the temptation that was growing when he was around her. The temptation to kiss her, to enjoy her giving nature. To make her his wife in every way.

Chapter Six

Molly hesitated, staring at her reflection in the mirror. She almost didn't recognize herself. She had slipped into the apartment earlier without seeing anyone. Using the guest bathroom, she prepared for the party. Now she was ready. Or as ready as she was going to get. Could she pull this off?

It wasn't really her. Just part of this weird dance she was doing with Kaliq. Her hair was a froth of curls, framing her face, softening it. Making her eyes look huge.

Or was it the new makeup the stylist had suggested? Molly wasn't sure, but she looked different. Mysterious, interesting, almost sexy.

The red lipstick matched her dress. As did her fingernails and toenails. The dress hadn't looked so blatantly sexy in the boutique, had it? Had she put on weight? Or had it been this skintight yesterday?

Swallowing hard and taking a deep breath, she wondered for the millionth time what Kaliq would say.

"No time like the present to find out," she said, taking another deep breath. Many more and she'd start to hyperventilate. Throwing open the door, she raised her head, threw back her shoulders and walked boldly out.

Down the hall, into the living room—her heart beating a rapid tempo.

Kaliq stood near the windows. He did that a lot, she noticed. Did he feel confined in buildings? Was he thinking about the desert again?

She must have made some noise, because he turned. And stared.

Almost smiling, Molly felt giddy with unexpected delight. After five years of working together, she'd finally surprised him.

"Molly?"

Sashaying into the room with a bravado she didn't feel, she nodded. "You said you liked my hair around my face, so I got it cut."

Darn, she hadn't meant to let that slip. That was not the reason she got her hair cut. She liked the short style and the loose curls that now framed her face. It was a sassy look, one she would never have tried before. But somehow it seemed right for tonight's event.

"Did I also say I liked you in red? What there almost is of that dress," he said, his gaze roving over every inch of her. Did he linger on certain areas?

The familiar flutter began. She needn't worry about being cold in the dress. The heat that swept through her at his look would keep her warm in a snowstorm.

"Not red particularly, but you did say you were tired of black. Are you ready to go?"

He hesitated for a long moment. Then nodded curtly.

"Hasim has the car down in front. Do you have a coat or something to wear with that?"

"Yes, it's by the door." Impulsively she stepped closer and reached up to pat his collar, brush an imaginary speck of lint from his shoulder. What was she trying to prove?

The edge of his hand lifted her chin. Kaliq lowered his head until his face was only inches from her, his breath caressing her cheeks. The dark glitter in his eyes had her pulse racing.

"What are you doing tonight, Molly?" he asked in a low husky voice.

A dozen answers trembled on her lips. She decided to go with honesty. "I'm trying to act the part of devoted wife of a worldly man," she said. Her lips seemed to tingle. Would he close those scant few inches and kiss her?

"Ah, I wondered."

Hé straightened and offered his arm. "Shall we?"

Disappointed, she hid it, smiling brightly.

The reception was in full swing by the time they arrived. A uniformed maid took Molly's coat. It was one thing to wear the dress in the safety of their apartment, but quite something else to walk into a room of strangers. For a long moment she hesitated at the entrance to the wide ballroom.

Molly had never been the belle of any ball, but for an instant she knew what it felt like. Men stopped and stared, smiles of appreciation lighting their features. Women discreetly assessed her dress and hairstyle. From some of the frowns, Molly wasn't sure if they disapproved or were envious. Raising her chin, she hoped she was equal to the task she'd set herself. She would hate herself in the morning if she made a fool of herself at Kaliq's expense.

Kaliq introduced her to their host, obtained a glass of ginger ale for her and gently steered her toward a group of men he wanted to speak with. Though his touch was light at the small of her back, Molly's skin heated and tingled. She tried to ignore the sensation and concentrated on making a good impression on his colleagues.

Greeting the men, some of whom she knew, she fell silent, content to listen to the conversation swirling around her without having to participate. It was an interesting topic, the latest international business trends. She would pick up points, which would assist in her job.

When Kaliq spoke, she noticed how often the others deferred to his opinions and seemed to value his input. She, too, valued his opinions, though she was more likely to argue with them when the occasion arose. He didn't want to surround himself with yes men, and Molly made sure she couldn't ever be counted as one.

"What about you, Molly? What is a woman's take on all this?" one of the men asked.

Thinking carefully before she spoke, Molly was gratified to find the same attention given her. Though one or two of the men obviously disagreed, no one contradicted her.

"And who is this fascinating creature who has the men hanging on her every word?" A tall statuesque blonde joined the group, her eyes surveying each man as if he was her special property. Smiling at Kaliq, she extended her hand. "I don't believe we've met. I'm Sally Rogers."

Kaliq shook her hand briefly. "Kaliq bin Shalik. My wife, Molly."

For a moment the blonde's confidence wavered, but she recovered quickly.

"How nice."

"It is for me," Molly said, stepping just a bit closer to Kaliq. She knew she couldn't compete with the women he used to date, but for now he was off-limits to all other women. And Molly meant for them to know it!

Startled at her action, she caught herself up. What was she doing, thinking of Kaliq as hers? Theirs was a business arrangement, a marriage to suit them both. Not some grand love affair that excluded the rest of the world.

Molly wondered what it would be like to be caught up in blazing passion and devoted love, as they were displaying to the world.

When Kaliq's hand rested on her bare shoulder, she almost jumped. Then she smiled and turned to him, hoping the confusion of her thoughts didn't show in her eyes.

"Would you care for something to eat?" he asked softly, turning slightly from the group.

"Yes, I'm starving."

"I've noticed how you enjoy your meals," he said as he excused them and headed for the lavish buffet set on tables at the far wall.

"I need to keep up my strength."

"Ah, eating for two, I believe the saying goes."

"Actually I was thinking more of keeping up with you. Do you think I came across too strongly in that group? I noticed a couple of the men seemed annoyed."

"You expressed yourself well. Morganstern didn't like your opinion, but you wouldn't let that stop you, would you?"

"No."

Kaliq spoke to several people in passing, and Molly wondered if he knew everyone present.

When another woman stopped him, Molly felt her heart sink. She'd thought Sally Rogers beautiful, but this woman made Sally look like a gauche high-school girl.

"Stunning" was the only term to describe her. Depressed, Molly watched while Kaliq's former wife greeted him.

"Hello, darling," the woman said, reaching up to kiss Kaliq with a familiarity that had Molly fisting her hands.

Kaliq stepped back, his expression impassive. "Sabrina. I didn't know you would be here."

"Obviously, darling. Justin thought it would be a nice diversion for us to attend. Have you seen the paintings Sven bought from his protégé? Intriguing work. I do believe he will be a huge success."

Sabrina let her gaze move to Molly. There was a tightness around the eyes, but beyond that, her smile seemed almost genuine.

"Molly, are you Kaliq's date for the evening?"

"No, Sabrina, Molly is my wife."

Her shocked look proved she had not heard about Kaliq's marriage. Molly felt a hint of smug satisfaction at the woman's startled expression.

Sabrina's gaze swung back to his. "You remarried?"

"I was free to do so."

"To her?" she asked as if Molly was totally beyond the realm of possibility.

Kaliq smiled at Molly, winking with his left eye. "To Molly. Wish us well, Sabrina. We're having a baby."

Shocked, Sabrina looked back and forth as if trying to fathom the words she'd heard.

"And my wife is hungry. If you'll excuse us." He took Molly's arm and continued on his way.

Molly could feel the tension shimmering in the air.

"She is still quite lovely," she murmured, feeling she ought to say something. The spurt of jealousy that gripped her hadn't abated. But there was nothing for her to be concerned about. It wasn't as if Kaliq had any interest in Sabrina. Or in her.

"I didn't know she would be here. Dammit, Sven knows I don't like to even be in the same room with her!"

"Who is Justin?"

"I don't know, her latest, I guess. I don't really care." Kaliq's anger simmered just below the surface. His control was too well entrenched for him to do anything foolish, but Molly could feel his fury.

"What would you like to eat?"

They had reached the buffet tables, and from the tone of his voice, Molly knew further conversation about his beautiful ex-wife was closed.

When they finished nibbling at some of the hors d'oeuvres, Kaliq introduced Molly to another couple and they chatted for a few minutes. Then one of the men Molly had met earlier joined them.

"Can I borrow Molly for a moment? Morganstern has finally come up with what he thinks are sound reasons to repute her views on that global trend. I want to see if Molly can defend herself.''

At Kaliq's nod she put down her glass and crossed the room. In only moments she was embroiled in a debate with the older man who didn't agree with her. Stretching her mental abilities, she countered all his arguments, stating hers forcefully and with conviction.

Soon the others in the group were laughing and rooting for her. The debate cooled and the topic changed.

Kaliq joined her.

''Pretty wife you've got there, Kaliq,'' one man said genially.

''Smart, too,'' Morganstern growled, not looking at all displeased.

''I agree. If you gentlemen will excuse us?'' He took Molly's hand, threading his fingers through hers.

When they were out of hearing, he glanced at her, anger once again simmering.

''I do not expect to find my wife flirting with other men at parties. It was unacceptable with Sabrina, and it is unacceptable with you!''

Shocked, Molly stopped and turned to face him. Her own indignation was immediate.

''Just a minute, I was not flirting with anyone!''

''And what was all that laughing at Morganstern's stupid jokes and exchanging amused glances with Peterson?''

''Which one was Peterson?''

''You don't even know the man's name, but you can flirt with him?''

''I hardly call being cordial at a party flirting.''

''And I hardly call it circumspect. What if the INS has an agent here? What would he think of our marriage?''

Narrowing her eyes, Molly studied Kaliq. "Let me guess. Knowing what little I do about Sabrina, I imagine she is the type to demand constant attention from the opposite sex. Are you suggesting that I'm at all like that? After having worked together, I would expect a bit more faith from you!"

"And what would you call your behavior?"

"Making a good impression so men will be envious of you for having married me," she said swiftly.

Slowly the tension faded from Kaliq's expression. He began to smile.

Molly's knees grew wobbly, her heart thudded in her chest, and she felt like she might melt into a puddle at Kaliq's feet. How could just a smile turn her bones to jelly and her mind to mush?

"And do all those men now envy me?"

She shrugged, looking away before she did something foolish like flinging herself into his arms and demanding he take them home so she could escape the stress of the party and the constant need to guard against making a major mistake.

"I only know what they think about the international banking situation and the recession in Japan. But I hope they think I'm more than some bit of fluff you picked up," she said with some asperity.

"Are we talking about Sabrina again?"

Hearing a hint of amusement in his voice, she dared another look in his direction. His dark eyes danced.

"If the shoe fits."

"Come, then, and let us mingle so more people here can meet you and be envious of my good fortune."

Molly knew Kaliq was teasing her, but she didn't mind. Despite her trepidation about the evening, she was having a wonderful time. Kaliq remained attentive throughout the rest of their evening, displaying all the pride of a newly married man. She tried not to wish it was true, instead of make-believe.

If she let herself forget for a single minute the reason for their union, Molly knew she could become swept away by the enigmatic man. His charm was deep and dangerous. Playing a part was only one step from living a part. And she was finding it more and more difficult to remember it was only a charade.

By the time they left, Molly was exhausted. If this was what she could expect when they went out, she'd do her best to see they stayed home as much as possible.

"Did you enjoy yourself?" Kaliq asked, one finger idly toying with a curl of her hair. They were sitting in the back of the limousine while Hasim drove swiftly through the dark streets.

"More than I thought I would. But I'm not much for big gatherings like that." She should be able to relax. The evening was behind her, and she had not made a single faux pas.

But how could anyone relax with Kaliq so close? With his fingers in her hair? His scent surrounding her?

"You handled yourself well. We will be obligated to attend a certain number of similar functions during the year. In future I will consult you before having Elise send an acceptance."

Molly smiled, despite the flutters his touch brought. "Thank you."

"I think being married to an American woman is going to be an interesting journey."

"Journey?"

"To our final destination."

"Which is?"

"That's part of the interesting aspect—we don't know the final destination yet."

Molly knew where an interim destination would be if Kaliq didn't stop touching her, toying with her hair. And tonight he had no work in the office to occupy his time!

But she wasn't ready for something like that. Until a few weeks ago, she'd thought herself in love with Chad. No, she *had* been in love with him. His deceit had killed it instantly. But it would be safer to go through life without the complications of falling for another man. Especially one who would never love her in return.

Even one as exciting as Kaliq.

Hadn't he said arranged marriages were not uncommon in his country? And they did well because of mutual respect and liking.

But did the brides in those kinds of marriages feel a breathlessness whenever their new husbands came close? Did their hearts pound and their senses flee?

Hasim delivered them to the door and drove off to park the car. Molly followed Kaliq into the elevator, her nerves stretched tighter every second as the car silently rose to their floor.

Kaliq let them into their apartment. On the table to the left Hasim had propped up a note. Kaliq took it as Molly shed her coat.

"Important?" she asked. Probably not, or Hasim would have mentioned it in the car.

"A message from my father," Kaliq said. He skimmed the words again and shrugged. "It seems Roeuk discovered our marriage and informed my father. He wishes to speak with me."

Molly almost giggled. She caught her lower lip between her teeth. Kaliq made it sound like he was a recalcitrant teenager about to be hauled on the carpet.

"I take it you didn't tell your parents," she said when the danger of the giggles had passed.

"Not as yet." He glanced at his watch. "It is morning there. I'll phone him now."

"Then I guess I'll head for bed."

Kaliq watched her hurry down the hall almost regretfully. He didn't want the night to end. He knew she'd be safely tucked into the bed before he finished his phone call. Either asleep or feigning sleep. Should he call her on it tonight? Talk to her in the dark, learn more about the woman than what he thought he knew from working with her?

After the way she attacked Morganstern's antiquated ideas, she could obviously hold her own in various situations. Yet she still acted like a skittish filly around him.

He'd let her get away with it tonight, but not forever. Pretending to be a devoted couple was wearing on a man, especially when his wife kept that bright smile trained in his direction. What would Molly do if he kissed her, ran his hands over that sexy body, felt the heat of her skin, the softness of its texture? Her hair felt like silk; how would her skin feel?

A man could only withstand so much temptation before giving in. And he'd been a long time without a woman. He wondered if he'd ever made love to such a contradiction of shyness and boldness. Her dress caused quite a stir tonight, yet the shy innocence that shone from her eyes was a direct challenge. One he wanted to take.

But first he needed to talk to his father. He knew the man would be disappointed he hadn't told him about his marriage. How Roeuk had discovered it was another question.

As Kaliq had suspected, his father was upset. He tried to explain the situation, but his father insisted there would have been other ways to comply with the American rules and regulations regarding the visa situation. He questioned his son's motive for marrying yet another foreigner.

"Did you not learn your lesson with Sabrina," Mohammad bin Shalik roared.

"Molly is different," Kaliq defended, keeping his voice low and calm. His father had a tendency to exaggerate everything, and Kaliq knew from years of experience that someone had to keep a cool head.

"I shall be the judge of that. Bring her here so I can meet her."

"Not just now, Father. If I could take a trip home without jeopardizing the negotiations, I would have returned to obtain a visa."

"How are the negotiations proceeding?" Diverted, he questioned his son on the progress with the union. It was only at the end of the conversation that he again ordered his son home—as soon as the negotiations were settled in their favor!

Kaliq hung up the phone and leaned back in his desk chair. Dealing with his father never got easier. The man was absolute ruler in his household, and getting him to change his mind about anything required a certain finesse Kaliq wondered if he'd ever master.

He should take lessons from his mother. She seemed to get whatever she wanted from her husband. Not that she ever asked for much. Maybe that was the key. Everything she asked for was important to her, and her husband was pleased to indulge her to bring her happiness.

What would bring Molly happiness? Kaliq wondered.

Separate bedrooms, he suspected, frowning.

A quick end to their mock marriage?

Three days of wedded bliss was not enough time to see how they would deal together in the future. He thought he knew her from the years she'd worked for him. Tonight, though, she had surprised him. Would there be other surprises?

Delightful ones or distressful ones?

The adventure of marriage was not something he had considered after divorcing Sabrina. He didn't like the games and the constant need to be on guard. But with Molly it would be different. Vastly different. And that held certain appeal.

Anticipating seeing her in the morning, he rose and headed for their room. He knew she'd be asleep, but just in case she wasn't...

Molly looked up from the toast she was buttering when Kaliq joined her in the dining room the next morning.

"Good morning," she said, carefully resuming her task. She'd been disappointed when she awoke to find Kaliq had already risen. Not that she expected him to stay in bed. Or care to be there when she awoke, she assured herself.

"Did you sleep well?" he inquired.

"Yes." She refused to meet his eyes.

Kaliq sat at the head of the table and poured himself some coffee. As if he'd been listening behind the door, Hasim entered with a plate of steaming-hot food. Molly wasn't sure she knew what it was and didn't care to ask. She still had problems with some foods due to her pregnancy.

"My cousin Roeuk and his wife have invited us to visit next weekend," Kaliq said when Hasim left.

"In Washington?"

"Yes. We can fly down next Saturday and return Sunday."

"That's a quick visit."

"You would prefer longer?"

"No, that's fine. I've met Roeuk. I look forward to meeting his wife."

"They are both anxious to get to know you."

Molly looked up at the tone in his voice. "In what way?"

"Just vetting a new wife," Kaliq said as he began to eat.

"Maybe I don't want to be vetted. You did tell them this is temporary," she said.

He looked at her. "Slipped my mind."

"Ha! Your mind is like a steel trap. Why didn't you tell them?"

"They don't need to know."

"What happens when we separate?"

Kaliq shrugged. "Whatever, they will deal with it then. Hasim had your furnishings moved here yesterday. Have you seen them?" he asked, changing the subject.

"He told me this morning the pieces are all in one room."

"So today we'll place them where you wish."

Mocking him gently, she inclined her head the way he did. "As you wish."

The glint in his eye told her he noticed and chose not to comment.

The day turned out to be fun for Molly. Neither Kaliq nor Hasim would allow her to lift anything. Once Hasim got over his astonishment that Kaliq planned to participate in the actual moving of the furniture, he grew more at ease in their presence, though never crossing the bounds of propriety.

Molly carefully studied each room and had a piece put where she thought it would enhance the existing arrangement. With various pieces of her furniture throughout, she felt more at home.

Two odd chairs remained. Studying them with a critical eye, she knew they would have to go.

"Sorry you moved these, Hasim. They are too tacky to stay."

"Tacky?"

"Ugly, unsuitable." She sighed and sat on one. "And uncomfortable. I don't know why I had them moved."

Hasim glided away as the doorbell rang. Molly looked at Kaliq.

"Are you expecting company? I look a mess."

"I'm not expecting anyone." He moved to the archway and listened.

"Ah, the Immigration inspector, if I'm not mistaken." He held out his hand and drew Molly to her feet. "Let's go be inspected."

The agent from INS stayed only an hour, looked into every aspect of the apartment and asked numerous questions—some of which had been asked at their offices just the previous morning.

When he left, he mentioned he thought everything was in order. There were a few more technicalities, but it looked in all likelihood that they would release the file for the resident visa.

Molly waited until the door closed behind him and then clapped her hands.

"We did it!"

"Perhaps. Did you notice he never quite said it was a done deal? When I have the green card, then we'll know we did it."

"I think it's a done deal. And you know what tipped the scales, don't you?" she asked sassily when Kaliq merely shrugged.

"What?"

"My looking terrible today. You'd have to love me to put up with this!"

He ran a fingertip along her cheek, tracing her jaw. "I would, would I?"

Closing the distance, he kissed her.

The unexpected embrace caught her unaware. Molly leaned back against the wall to keep from falling. After her initial surprise, she began to savor the feel of Kaliq's lips against hers, relished the sensations that cascaded through her. She opened her lips to respond and was swept away in a vortex of sensations and swirling excitement.

When he straightened, she gazed up into his dark eyes, glad for the support of the wall, wondering if he could hear the thundering of her heart. What was he thinking? Did the kisses mean anything? Or was it just for the moment? Was she just convenient?

"Even though he reported it looks likely he would release the file for visa processing, I say we continue our vigilance until it is in hand," Kaliq said slowly, lightly tracing her jaw with a finger. He met her gaze and cocked an eyebrow. "I believe we need to keep up the devoted-couple bit—to fool the INS, of course."

"I think they are fooled," she said. "And I doubt they'll be back here again."

"Ah, you wish to make some change?"

Restlessly she pushed away and paced the room. "I don't think we need to continue sharing a bed. I can leave my clothes in the closet for a while, but we've been questioned twice. Do you really think they will do it again?" Not meeting his eyes, she rubbed her arms and continued to pace.

The truth was, she wasn't sure she could resist the strong pull of attraction being around Kaliq provoked. She had managed to slip off to bed before him for a couple of nights, but how long could she keep it up? How long before she rolled over in the night and snuggled against his strong body? How long could she resist temptation before throwing caution to the wind and asking him to kiss her? To make love to his wife?

And what would happen if she was still wide awake when he joined her in that bed? Even though it was large, it wasn't that large. Look at how big the room was, yet she was acutely aware of Kaliq's every move.

Risking a quick look, she found his expression bland. What did he think of her demand?

"Your choice," he said. Abruptly he turned and left the room.

"Well, Molly, you got what you wanted," she murmured, wondering why she felt so disappointed.

Chapter Seven

Molly gazed out the airplane window as the tall spire of the Washington Monument came into view. She glanced at Kaliq. He was still engrossed in one of the reports he'd brought along to study. Turning back to the small window, she wondered what this visit would bring. Would Roeuk grill her on why she'd married his cousin? Find her lacking in the attributes the family would wish for Kaliq's wife? She knew it was a temporary arrangement, but Kaliq's family did not. Or had Kaliq told Roeuk the reason for their hasty wedding? Would they be disappointed in his choice for a wife?

She hoped not. She wanted his family to like her.

The week just past had been odd. During the day she had felt no different from how she'd felt for the past five years. Except for a strong sense of awareness of Kaliq that had never been present before. She hoped she had hidden that from him, but with his uncanny ability to cut to the heart of the matter in business dealings, she worried she'd given herself away.

The evenings had been a different story. Those they spent together. Awkwardly at first, like strangers trying to grope their way through the stages of learning about one another. But as the week progressed, Molly knew she'd learned more about her enigmatic husband than she'd gleaned over all the years they'd worked together.

And what little she had learned confused her.

Kaliq was a curious blend of his Arabian heritage and Western ways. While he paid lip service to women's rights, Molly suspected if he could have things entirely his way, his word would be law.

To that end, she found herself challenging him over inconsequential things just for the impish joy of watching him as he drew on his strength of resolve and marshaled his arguments.

By Thursday he'd caught her out.

Molly smiled dreamily as she gazed at the approaching airport. He'd been furious! Or had that been just for her benefit? She still thought she'd seen a twinkle of amusement in his dark eyes for all his arguments.

But the kisses he'd showered on her had not been amusing. Exciting, tumultuous, wildly exotic, but definitely not amusing! She grew warm remembering. If Hasim had not interrupted, would those kisses have led to something more?

Sometimes she regretted making an issue of moving into her own room after Immigration's home inspection. Not that she expected anything from her husband. He'd not touched her the two nights she'd shared that huge bed. Would her remaining there have changed anything?

Did she really want to change things? It wasn't as if their marriage was real or they planned to continue it.

A physical intimacy would complicate matters, she knew. But that knowledge didn't stop her yearning. Just for a kind word, a gentle caress. A passionate kiss.

Be grateful for what you have, she scolded herself.

Kaliq had offered her the protection of his name, which was more than she should have ever expected. For that she would forever be grateful.

But sometimes she wished she had not told him about Chad. Wished that she had not had to get married. Even fantasized once or twice that they had married because of mutual desire. Though their marriage was unconventional, she liked it.

What would it be like if Kaliq had wooed her and won her? Courted her with flowers, dinners out, dancing? Pledged himself to her for all time?

She shook her head and sighed. He had made his position on women clear enough. He didn't trust them. And she was realistic enough to know that if his visa had not lapsed, he would never have thought of marrying her—or anyone else.

After seeing Sabrina, she wondered how much the woman regretted the loss of Kaliq. Did she wish to find a way to rekindle his affections? Or had it been a mercenary arrangement from the beginning?

How could she not be attracted to the man? And regret the ending of their relationship? Molly couldn't imagine being more interested in Kaliq's fortune than the man himself.

"Well, she can't have him," Molly murmured, startled by the strength of her feelings.

"What?" Kaliq looked at her.

"Nothing. I was just thinking aloud. We're almost there." She kept her gaze firmly out the window, lest he suspect what she'd said. She needed to watch her tongue!

He slid the papers back into the file and placed it into his briefcase. When he placed it beneath the seat in front of him, Molly turned to watch.

"Did the Alderon report have what you were looking for?" she asked. The small firm was a subsidiary of ALK Shipping and recently acquired.

"The returns are higher than expected."

"Which means Johnson is doing a good job there. I know you had doubts when you gave him the manager's position."

"It's early yet. But yes, I think he's demonstrating more potential than I originally expected." Kaliq raised an eyebrow. "Are you going to say you told me so?"

Molly grinned. "Why, Kal, I didn't know you thought I was the type to gloat when proved right."

"Proved right? You voiced approval of Johnson's appointment, but the proof is far from in."

"The way you go, it'll be fifty years before you let yourself admit he's a good choice."

"I believe in accepting responsibility for my decisions, however they turn out."

"I hope you never regret any of them," she said, glancing at her wedding band.

"If you are referring to our marriage, I accept responsibility for that, as well. Time will tell if it proves successful."

"Do we wait fifty years to find out?" Molly almost slapped her hand over her mouth after the words came out. She stared at him wide-eyed. It sounded too much like she wanted to stay married. It was one thing to fantasize about being courted, and quite another to verbalize it!

Kaliq's expression changed almost imperceptibly, became more guarded. "We could wait fifty years. Are you considering staying with me that long?"

For a moment she was speechless as the realization flooded. She *did* want to stay with him! She liked and respected him. If she was totally honest, she had enjoyed the week and a half they'd been married. She knew she could depend on him to do the right thing, no matter what the cost to himself. He would see to it that he was a good reliable husband. Someone she could count on.

But how did he feel?

For a wild giddy moment, Molly considered the possibility of staying married. Could they make it work? The romantic sheik and the plain personal assistant from Ohio?

Slowly reality intruded. Even if they continued, she didn't want a lopsided relationship, with her growing fonder and fonder of Kal while he continued his own way.

"We'll see," she temporized, afraid of the sudden suspicion that plagued her. She was growing too fond of her boss. Too intrigued with the idea of staying with him for the rest of her life. Too involved with watching him when he didn't know she was looking, listening to him as if she'd never heard him before. And she was growing too dependent. Time to distance herself. Hadn't she learned her lesson?

Yet Kaliq was unlike any other man she'd ever known. There was an innate honesty and honor about the man. Almost old-worldly. A blend of the cultures maybe. But captivating and comforting. She knew beyond any doubt he would live up to his word. He would never lie or deceive someone—especially someone he cared about.

She couldn't be falling in love with him! This was just a rebound thing or something. She couldn't fall in love again. It was too risky for her heart.

And with someone like Kaliq, even more so.

Yet...

The plane bumped gently down.

"Oh, we're here already," Molly said, glad of the interruption to her tumbling thoughts. "You never told me—what should I call your cousin? Your Excellency? Or Emir? Or do you have another form of address I should use?" she asked, her concerns switching to the forthcoming visit.

How would she fit in with Kaliq's family? Would they all know instantly she was a fraud?

Kaliq laughed softly. "Call him Roeuk—he's your cousin now, too. And his wife is Megan, his daughter is Norrie and his son is Sam."

"Sam?" Molly frowned. That didn't sound very Arabian to her.

"Actually his full name is Hanid Pierre bin Shalik. Roeuk's mother is French. But for some reason unbeknownst to me, they have called him Sam since his birth."

Feeling a bit shy and out of place, Molly followed Kaliq up the jetway and into the airport concourse. Roeuk, tall and imposing, stood to one side waiting. Molly couldn't help comparing the two men. Both had the same way of carrying themselves as if they had no equal. Their self-confidence was amazing, almost arrogant. But they were sexy and charming nonetheless.

The cousins greeted each other rather formally, Molly thought, but forgot it when Roeuk turned to her

and smiled. He inclined his head in a manner similar
to Kaliq.

"Welcome to our family, Molly bin Shalik. You
honor us with this marriage."

"Thank you." Flustered, she looked to Kaliq for
support. She felt awful with their charade. How would
Roeuk feel when the truth all came out?

To Molly's surprise, there was no chauffeur. Roeuk
drove. The luxurious Mercedes was a delight. Molly
sat alone in the back while the two men sat in the front
and conversed quickly. She ran her hand lovingly over
the rich leather and sighed in contentment. She'd better
not grow too used to such luxury, she thought, but it
was nice while it lasted.

When Roeuk turned into a short driveway some time
later, the house was not what she expected. Instead of
a huge mansion surrounded by acres of manicured
lawns, the modest ranch bungalow sat in the center of
an ordinary middle-class neighborhood. She expected
something more palatial.

Even Kaliq seemed surprised.

"You live here?"

Roeuk raised an eyebrow. "You have a problem
with my home?"

"No. Just…it's different from your villa in Manasia."

"This was Megan's home before we married. And
it's becoming crowded now. But when we first married,
I don't think she quite trusted it would last and wanted
something of her own as insurance. Now we're used
to it. We are not in the States that much to make an
issue of it. But when the baby comes, we'll definitely
need something larger."

"Megan's expecting again?" Kaliq asked as he climbed from the car and held the back door for Molly.

At Roeuk's nod, he looked at Molly. "Something else you will have in common with Megan."

"The first thing being?" Molly asked, flicking a glance at Kaliq. He'd told his cousin she was pregnant? Had he told him the full circumstances?

"Being married to a foreign national, of course."

"And both to men from a very chauvinistic society," Molly mused, already growing used to Kaliq's orders, instead of requests. She'd decided from the first to remember it was his way.

He leaned close so only she could hear. "Isn't that the natural order of things? For a man to rule and a woman to see to his needs?"

Her chin jutting, Molly glared at him. "In your dreams!"

He smiled broadly. "Ah, as you say, in my dreams."

"Kaliq! How nice to see you again!" A tall woman and a teenage girl, looking remarkably alike, smiled broadly as they moved to greet him.

Kaliq straightened and, taking Molly's hand in his, walked forward to meet Megan and Norrie.

"You have grown another six inches, I am sure, since I last saw you," Kaliq said as he gave the girl a hug, then held her away from him to study her.

"No, but I'm losing some of that baby fat, so I look taller, don't I, Daddy?" she asked her father.

Roeuk exchanged an amused glance with his wife and nodded.

"And this must be Molly. I'm Megan, Roeuk's wife. I'm so glad you came! We'll have a great weekend. Come on in. The baby's asleep, but he'll be awake soon and I need to listen for him. How was your trip?"

"Fine." Molly was swept along with their enthusiasm. Some of her nervousness faded. Maybe the weekend would go all right, after all. She glanced over her shoulder. Kaliq and Roeuk stood by the car, their voices low as they talked. Following Megan, Molly was pleased that Norrie kept pace with her.

"Kaliq said you lived right in Manhattan before you got married. Don't you love New York? I think the stores there would offer a ton of cool things," Norrie said excitedly. "We've been only once. Maybe you and Kaliq would invite me up to visit."

Megan laughed and chided her daughter. "They don't want company just yet. I already told you we would stop there before heading for home."

"That's weeks away," she said, wrinkling her nose. "Kaliq said you were pregnant—did you know my mom's pregnant, too?" Norrie asked as they entered the house. "I'm hoping for a girl this time, but Mom says all she cares about is that it's a healthy child. And she won't find out ahead of time. Do you know what you're having yet?"

Molly shook her head. With a start she realized she hadn't thought much about the baby beyond being pregnant. Of course, the past week had been taken up with Kaliq. But in only a few months she'd be a mother with a baby totally dependent upon her.

Would she still be married to Kaliq? Or would they have ended their marriage by then? Once he received his green card, the need to remain married would end. How long would that take? she wondered.

She didn't want to end it. Didn't want to be on her own, coping with work and a baby and the loneliness. Susan would not want a baby to share their small apartment. During the past week, Molly had found she liked sitting in the evenings talking, listening to music and relaxing in a living room that was so different from what she was used to.

She'd miss that when their arrangement ended.

"Hush, Norrie, let Molly get her breath. Do you wish to freshen up after your flight? I'll show you where you'll be staying tonight." Megan led the way down a short hall.

"Roeuk says we have to get a larger place when the baby comes. This is only a three-bedroom house. Here, you and Kaliq will have Norrie's room for the night." Megan paused at the doorway of a light airy room. The bed was covered with an organdy spread that matched the curtains on the windows.

It was a teenager's room with all the things a young girl cherished—from a purple stuffed animal on one shelf to posters of movie stars pinned to the walls. But Molly didn't notice the decorations—she focused on the bed.

The small double bed.

This was nothing like the king-size bed Kaliq had in his bedroom. This one looked scarcely large enough for two people to squeeze in without falling to the floor.

Molly felt a touch of panic. She had barely made it through two nights with Kaliq with acres of room between them. In this tiny bed she'd get no sleep, no rest. She couldn't do it!

"Is something wrong?" Norrie asked.

Molly dragged her gaze away from the bed and tried to smile at the teenager.

"Everything is fine. Your room is lovely. I just hate for you to give it up for us."

She had to talk to Kaliq. Maybe they could stay in a hotel nearby—so as not to force Norrie from her room. That would be a strong enough reason. They could still spend all the time he wanted with Roeuk and Megan.

"It's no big deal. Besides, I'm staying with Stephie tonight. She's my best friend."

"We'll leave you alone. Come out when you are ready," Megan said, taking her daughter's arm and pulling her into the hall. "I'll fix something cold to drink."

"Thanks, I won't be long," Molly said, still standing near the door. She heard the men's voices and wondered if she could get Kaliq alone. Before she could formulate a way, he walked into the bedroom carrying their cases.

Molly moved swiftly, closing the door and leaning against it.

"Kaliq, we can't stay here."

He calmly put the cases on the floor near the bed and surveyed the room. "Is there a problem?"

"Look at that bed!"

No, that wasn't what she wanted to say. She cleared her throat. "I mean, this is Norrie's room. She's having to sleep at a friend's while we're here. If we stayed at a hotel, she wouldn't be forced out of her room."

"Stay at a hotel?"

"Yes. We could book a room nearby. Still see all you want of Roeuk and Megan and then…" Her voice trailed off at his expression.

"I would never offend my cousin in such a way," Kaliq said firmly.

"Offend?"

"To throw his hospitality back in his face."

She took a breath to counter his argument, then slowly let it out. Leaving for a hotel would smack of rejecting their hospitality. Nervously she glanced at the bed again.

"That's a small bed."

"If you are worried about falling out in the night, I'll hold you to make sure that doesn't happen."

Visions of being wrapped in Kaliq's arms did nothing to quell the trepidation she felt. They only exacerbated the tingling sense of anticipation.

"No, I won't fall out." Or if she did, she'd just stay on the floor, where she'd be safe from temptation.

How could she tell him she wasn't worried about him being there, but about her reaction to him?

Obviously she could never even hint at such a thing! Maybe she could stay up all night. Or maybe between now and bedtime she would lose the fascination she had for Kaliq. Stop being so aware of his every movement, become more comfortable around him.

Comfortable? She felt as if she were on tenterhooks all the time!

Twenty minutes later Molly sat on the patio behind the house with Megan and Norrie. Two-year-old Sam toddled around the grassy yard, chasing after a ball his older sister kept throwing. The two men had gone off somewhere.

Sipping the fruit punch Megan had prepared, Molly tried to relax. There was nothing she could do about the sleeping arrangements but make the best of them. And try to get to bed before Kaliq.

They had agreed to a platonic marriage. Except for a few kisses, he had given her no indication he wanted to change that. And she fully remembered his scathing denunciation of his ex-wife. Molly needed to prove to Kaliq that he could trust her. Trust her to abide by the rules of their unconventional marriage.

"Sam is adorable," she said, watching the toddler's antics. Again she thought about her own baby. Would she have a little boy who would always be exploring and taking chances? Or maybe a daughter, with whom she could share so much. Megan and Norrie seemed very close. Molly would like that.

"Thanks. He's his dad all over."

"Like me?" Norrie asked.

"Yes, just like you. Both of you have Roeuk's stubborn streak."

Molly was puzzled. Hadn't Kaliq said Megan and Roeuk married only four years ago?

"You're not exactly a marshmallow yourself, Mom," Norrie teased.

"But it gets wearing standing up for myself all the time!"

Norrie laughed. "Like you don't have Daddy wrapped around your little finger."

"He's a totally frustrating, domineering, *infuriating* man!"

"And here I was going to ask you for advice on dealing with Kaliq," Molly said.

"Let me guess—he's also dictatorial, demanding and expects everyone to do his bidding without complaint," Megan said, her eyes dancing with amusement.

"You have known him a long time."

Megan laughed softly. "No, but he is very like Roeuk. Unless I stand up to him."

"That's why we come back to the States every year, right, Mom? To keep Daddy in line."

Megan made a mock expression of horror and looked around as if searching for her husband. "Shh, don't give away our secrets."

Norrie giggled and explained to Molly, "It's really different in Manasia. There're things I like, such as our home. It's huge and right on the water. I have a super room with a balcony. It even has stairs that lead to the garden. And we have tons of servants. I wouldn't even have to make my bed, except Mom makes me most days. Which our maid, Alyia, thinks is totally wrong."

"To be sure you know how. And Alyia knows how I feel," Megan interposed.

"Yeah, like I need to learn that."

"An old argument," Megan told Molly.

"And then we come here and do everything ourselves," Norrie continued. "But living there is more restrictive than here. For girls, anyway."

"And women," Megan said pensively. "It's a really progressive country for an Arab nation, but generations of traditions aren't going to change in a decade."

"Tell me about Manasia," Molly said. If the negotiations had not been so important, would Kaliq have acquiesced to his father's demands and returned home to introduce his new bride?

The descriptions Megan and Norrie shared were similar to those Kaliq had given her. It sounded like paradise. Though the restriction on women gave her pause. What would it be like for an American woman used to doing anything she wanted to live in such a society?

She asked Megan.

"For the most part, living there is wonderful. Of course, being married to Roeuk has a lot to do with that," she replied with a smile. "Because Roeuk is the titular head of Manasia, and because I am an American, I'm allowed a bit more freedom than most women. But I still chafe under the rules of the society sometimes."

"So we visit with Grandmère in France when she goes and come here every year," Norrie finished.

"But I doubt you'll live there," Megan said. "Kaliq seems quite dedicated to the shipping lines, and from what Roeuk has said, likes living in New York. It's different for us. Roeuk has to live there."

"We've never talked about going to Manasia," Molly said.

Of course not, theirs was a marriage of convenience that could end at any time. There was no reason for Molly to ever visit Manasia.

Yet she couldn't help but long to see Kaliq on the desert he loved. To watch him ride the wind. She bet he became one with his mount and could challenge everyone on horsemanship. His face would blaze with happiness and that heart-melting smile would be visible for miles.

What would it be like to sleep beneath a canopy of stars in a lavish tent, with carpets on the sand, and only the two of them in the vast expanse of the Arabian desert?

Megan looked at her seriously. "Kaliq would never make you live where you are unhappy. And there are a lot of wonderful aspects of living in Manasia, as you'll see when you two go to visit."

Nodding without saying a word, Molly longed to change the subject. She was still confused about how she felt. Was she falling in love with her husband?

As she sat in the shade of a huge old tree talking quietly with Roeuk's wife, Molly suddenly knew she never wanted to end their marriage. She wanted Kaliq on whatever terms he set. Lopsided marriage or not, she loved him!

He'd scoff if she ever told him. Hadn't she married

him to save face? To avoid becoming an unwed mother? He would never believe she'd fallen in love. Cynical and distrusting, Kaliq would forever question her motives if she confessed her love. Better to keep it a deep secret. Even if it meant leaving, she didn't want to give him cause to ever doubt her.

Dinner was entertaining. Molly laughed at the constant teasing between Roeuk and Megan, and noted some similarities to the ways she'd challenged Kaliq the past week. He watched the banter quietly, occasionally meeting her gaze, as if trying to divine her thoughts on the situation.

Norrie went to her friend's house right after supper, leaving the adults in the living room with their coffee. Molly tried to enjoy the evening, but the closer the time came to go to bed, the more nervous she became.

Stop it, she chided herself. She could control herself around her husband. He had never exceeded the bounds of propriety, and she wouldn't, either!

But it was the yearning that had her wanting more.

She tried to focus on the conversation, something about Kaliq getting a house in Manasia now that he was married again. But the words drifted by as her thoughts churned.

What would it be like to visit his country? To see the house Kaliq had grown up in, to meet his parents?

Would his father be furious he'd married another foreigner? His first marriage had not been a success. Did he dare admit this one was not, either?

"Molly?"

She looked at Megan. "Yes?"

"You haven't heard a word we've said. Are you tired? Would you like to go to bed? Don't stay up with us if you need to get some rest. I'm always so tired during the first few months of being pregnant. We'd all understand.''

Molly jumped up, snatching the excuse like a life-line.

''I am a bit tired.''

Kaliq rose, as well. ''We have tomorrow to continue our visit. I'll go with Molly.''

''Oh, you don't have to. I'm tired, so I will probably go right to sleep. Stay and visit with your cousin. I'll be fine. Really.''

The amusement in his eyes told her he wasn't fooled by her statement. He knew!

''I'm tired after the hectic week we spent,'' he said. ''Being married can wear a man out.''

She grew warm as Roeuk and Megan exchanged smiles. Head held high, she bid them good-night and headed for their room.

When the door was closed behind them, she rounded on Kaliq. ''Do you know what they thought after that statement?''

He began to unbutton the top button on his dress shirt. Pausing, he looked at her. ''Who?''

''Roeuk and Megan. Saying being married can wear a man out—they probably think we've been making love all night, every night so you can't get any sleep!''

He nodded and continued to unbutton his shirt. Molly watched as more and more of his chest was revealed. Her heart rate sped up, and her breathing grew shallow. He was a beautiful man, strong, sleek, male.

And she was in love with him.

How would it feel to touch that bronzed skin, feel the heat, run her fingertips over the contours, to let her lips and tongue taste him, caress him?

She spun around, then felt stupid staring at the door. "I need the bathroom," she said, and almost ran from the room.

"You are acting eight, not twenty-eight," she admonished herself when alone. Splashing water on her face, she quickly brushed her teeth and drew a deep breath. Another. Gradually her rioting senses calmed.

"I can do this," she told her reflection.

She could go into that room, get ready for bed while Kaliq used the bathroom and sleep in the bed. They had already proved it was possible to sleep and nothing else. She'd turn her back on him, make sure her hands stayed firmly away from his tantalizing skin and go right to sleep!

Feigning sleep when Kaliq returned to the room a few minutes after she'd dashed off her clothes and jumped beneath the covers didn't fool him for an instant. Resolutely she kept her eyes tightly shut, her hands in fists.

He switched off the lights and climbed into his side of the bed.

She wondered if she could breathe.

"Do you like Megan?" he asked, making no effort to be quiet.

Molly debated for a moment whether to answer or not. But he knew she wasn't asleep.

"Yes. She and I hit it off instantly. Sometimes that happens."

"They didn't have an easy time of it," he said, moving, settling in.

Molly froze, what was he doing? The mattress moved again and she felt the warmth of his leg beside her. Scant inches separated them. How could she be expected to sleep with him so tantalizingly close?

"What do you mean?" she asked. Talking would be good. She could concentrate on Kaliq's deep tones and maybe fall asleep that way.

Though she instantly felt wide awake and not the least bit sleepy.

"They were sweethearts during college, then my uncle had Roeuk brought home. Neither he nor Megan knew she was pregnant. By the time he tried to reach her, she'd left college to support herself and soon-to-be-born baby—Norrie."

"So they did just get married four years ago," she murmured.

"He was on a mission to the United States and saw her. It wasn't easy. They had been lovers in college. For ten years she'd thought he'd abandoned her. And when he found her again, he thought she'd run away to another man. It's hard to rebuild trust once it's been shattered."

"They seem perfect for each other. And both children are precious."

"Come closer, Molly, I want to talk to you." Kaliq slipped his arm beneath her neck and brought her up against his hard body.

Instantly heat cascaded through Molly. She could hardly breathe. How could she talk? His body was hard against the softer curves of her own. His scent seemed to invade every cell. Bracing herself, she found her hand pushed against his chest. She could feel the slow steady beat of his heart.

"About?" One word. If she could say one word, she could say more. At least she hoped so. Right now all she could do was concentrate on the sensations that swept through her. His arm beneath her neck, her head resting against his shoulder. The heat beneath the sheet that enveloped them both. His steady pulse while hers was racing.

She drew a shaky breath, filled with Kaliq's unique scent. Her heart skidded, raced.

"About you and me. So far only the two of us and your former roommate know the true circumstances of our marriage. I want our situation to stay that way. At least until I see my father. I will tell him the truth, of course."

"You didn't tell Roeuk?"

"No. But I suspect he's guessed. I will tell my parents when next I see them. By then I expect we shall have resolved our future."

She drew another shaky breath. By the time he returned home to visit, their marriage could be over.

Except she didn't want it to be over.

But what did Kaliq want?

Chapter Eight

Kaliq felt Molly's hand on his chest and everything inside him tightened. It was dark, quiet. He was alone in bed with a woman who was his wife. They had agreed to a platonic relationship, which had suited him when they made their unlikely bargain.

Now, however, he wanted to change the rules. Holding an armful of sweet femininity and doing nothing was almost more than a red-blooded man could tolerate. He wanted to bury himself in her, taste the sweet honey of her mouth, feel her satiny skin warm to his touch. Hear her soft cries of pleasure as they explored the heights of passion together.

But would Molly join him in that exploration? Or run screaming from the room?

If she remained, she'd probably expect some declaration of love. Wasn't that something all women wanted? Even if it was only said in the heat of passion?

And that he couldn't say.

He didn't believe in the emotion. It was simply

words women used to cover up the baser instincts such as greed and self-serving manipulation.

He'd thought he'd found love with Sabrina, only to discover the woman he had believed she was never existed. Learning from that, Kaliq knew women wanted to bind men in the throes of passion in order to get what they wanted—material things, power or prestige.

What did Molly want?

To be the strongest in a negotiation, a man needed to know what his opposition's goals were. What was important, what was not.

The key with Molly would be her baby.

Feeling her fingers flex against his chest almost clouded his mind enough to forget where he was. He grasped her hand, holding it tightly in his to keep her from distracting him.

"If we continue as we have this past week, I see no reason to terminate this marriage once the green card is issued. We deal well together. And with Hasim to help, you could continue to work after your baby is born, if you wished. Or stay home until the child begins school," he said, testing the waters.

She was silent. He wondered what thoughts milled around in her mind. She constantly surprised him. Was it because she had been on her own so long she didn't react as he expected women to do? Or was she just cleverer than Sabrina had been?

"I know you're not asleep. If my suggestion is too abhorrent to consider, just say so." He hadn't expected to feel impatient, frustrated that she hadn't instantly jumped at the opportunity to remain in the marriage.

"No, no, Kaliq, it's not abhorrent at all. You caught me by surprise. I mean, why me?"

"Why you what?"

"You could marry anyone in the world. Why settle for me?"

"First of all, I cannot marry anyone else right now—I'm already married. And second, I'm not 'settling' for anyone. We have worked well together professionally. I think we can forge a strong partnership in our personal lives, as well."

She didn't answer immediately.

His impatience grew. His suggestion didn't need that much consideration. She should know by now if she wanted to stay married or not. It wasn't as if she had other alternatives. Should he remind her of that?

"If you are worried about your baby, I'll be as good a father as I can for the child."

"But the baby isn't yours."

He was silent. Did she think he could not grow to care for a child just because it was not his? The child was hers. He liked her. Ergo, he could grow to like the child.

"I care for Norrie and Sam. They are not mine."

"I meant, wouldn't you like a child of your own?"

"Are you offering?"

Silence again. He frowned into the night, wishing she'd open that sassy mouth and tell him what she thought and what she thought he should think, as she'd done several nights last week. Maybe he should make it an order, rile her up to force an honest reaction.

"Molly, that's not something you have to decide right now. It's a moot point for several months. We can reevaluate the situation later. The issue at hand is whether to continue this marriage or not."

"I like being married to you," she said so softly he almost missed the words. But he heard them. And the depth of feeling that settled over him was unexpected.

"But I'm not sure we suit," she added.

"Let me be the one to decide that. You suit me fine. You are undemanding, are not grasping and greedy, and still have one of the finest business minds I deal with."

"Gee, how romantic."

"Romance doesn't play a part in this. We would go on as we started."

"Very well, Kaliq. If you are sure."

Despite her words, he heard the hesitation, the uncertainty. Time would prove him right. They would have a stable business marriage. And tied to him legally, she couldn't leave. He would keep his personal assistant and continue building ALK Shipping until it was the largest shipping line in the world.

Normally the finalizing of a deal called for a handshake. But Kaliq had no intention of shaking his wife's hand. Instead, he pulled her up across his chest and kissed her, threading his fingers into her soft bouncy curls, relishing the sensations that exploded through his body. Her feminine body rested on his strength. Her mouth opened to his, enticing him with its honey-hot sweetness. Her hands delved into his hair and caressed him, while one silky leg slipped between his. He wanted more, but it was too soon.

Lust grew, passion built. But, afraid to alarm her, he eased his ardor. He planned to do his seduction of her slowly. Until he had her bound to him in all the ways he could devise, he wanted nothing to scare her off.

Molly was different from Sabrina. Special. And someone he could envision living with until he grew old.

But with his blood thundering through his veins, he was hard-pressed to muster the control necessary to slow down. One hand swept across her back, feeling her muscles move beneath her cotton gown. Unable to resist, he filled his palm with the softness of her bottom. He wanted more, wanted to delve into the heat at her core, to take all the ardor she possessed and lavish it on himself.

With monumental effort, he moved his hand. Brought their kiss to an end.

Pleased to know she was breathing as hard as if she'd run a race, Kaliq had to satisfy himself with that. Progress sometimes comes one step at a time.

"When we return to New York, we'll have to begin searching for baby furniture," he said. A safe topic, one guaranteed to cool his hunger.

It wasn't what he wanted to talk about. He wanted to talk about making love to his wife. But not until she was ready. And he needed to make sure of her before moving to the next step.

Kaliq remembered the difficult tests of endurance he explored as a teenager and younger man. In the desert, dependent on only his own skills and expertise to keep himself alive, he fought a grueling duel against the relentless heat and blazing sun, and this had forged a strength that surprised him. In the endless miles of windswept sand, the taxing tests pitted his fledgling skills against the best of his father's warriors.

Yet in retrospect, it seemed easy in comparison to holding on to his self-control tonight. His body craved Molly's. His mouth continued to hunger for the taste of hers. His control was sorely tested as he gazed into the blackness and willed himself to keep his arm from tightening, to keep from throwing everything to the wind and claiming her.

It was a long time before he slept.

* * *

Molly was more confused than ever when they returned on Sunday. Standing at the large window in the living room of their apartment, she gazed sightlessly out at the darkness. It was after ten, and she was alone, except for Hasim, who was in his quarters.

The weekend had gone well. Roeuk seemed pleased his cousin had remarried. Megan welcomed her warmly. And she had loved Norrie and Sam. It was the thought of their deception that still lay heavily on her. That and the abandonment of her husband.

Kaliq had dropped her off on their return to New York that afternoon and headed for the office. Negotiations resumed in the morning, and he wanted to review some critical files.

Or at least that was what he told her.

Not that she didn't believe him, but he could have reviewed them early in the morning. If he needed to at all. His mind never seemed to forget a single fact. What did he need to examine now?

She noticed her reflection in the glass. Her hair waved around her face, softening her features. Her figure was still slim, showing only the slightest hint of the changes to come.

He had said last night he wanted to extend their marriage. She knew she hadn't dreamed that.

Had she?

Turning, she wandered over to the divan and sank down beside the book she'd brought to read. As if her mind could concentrate on anything.

Kaliq had treated her like a stranger today.

She had expected on waking this morning to find a new closeness between them. Something to show they would be able to forge a strong bond that would bind them through the years. A suggestion that he looked on her as more than just a personal assistant he didn't wish to lose.

Careful not to give any sign of the love that threatened to overwhelm her, she was content to take tiny steps forward until Kaliq might grow comfortable with their change of status.

Instead, he had been formal, cool, polite and distant.

Except for the blazing memories of his kisses, of the sensations she experienced when his hands caressed her as she rested against his strong chest, she might have thought she imagined last night.

Was this his way of advancing their marriage? One step forward, two back?

What did he want from her?

"Probably just a barrier between him and all the women who chase him," she muttered, frowning. Jumping to her feet, she paced to the window again.

"I could have gone to the office with him," she said to her reflection.

"Indeed you could have," Kaliq said from the doorway.

She spun around.

"In fact, I should have had you join me. I had the devil's own time finding some of the cargo manifests I wanted to use as examples." Kaliq walked calmly into the room, scarcely giving her a glance.

"They are in a file in Elise's area," she said, finding it difficult to switch into efficient assistant mode when her recent thoughts had nothing to do with business.

"I located them. I wish to leave early in the morning. If you can't be ready, I'll have Hasim return to pick you up."

Molly nodded. "I can be ready as early as you like."

If nothing else, she prided herself on her professionalism and devotion to her job. She was good at it, as he well knew.

How could she make herself equally indispensable in his personal life?

"I knew I could count on you." He glanced at his watch.

Stubbornly refusing to take the bait, Molly remained silent, watching. Feasting on him with her eyes. He looked tired. The lines around his eyes suggested strain.

She shouldn't be surprised. The negotiations were a huge responsibility. If they could get their terms, or close to them, it would make a monumental difference to their rate structures. Which would lead to more business. Expansion was the name of the game, and he was looking to increase revenues with the recent acquisition of the Alderon Company.

She wished she could offer some assurance that everything would turn out the way he wanted.

She crossed to pick up her book, to hide her expression. She almost laughed aloud. Imagine Kaliq needing any kind of assurance or comfort. The man was indomitable. He certainly didn't need platitudes from a personal assistant.

Or a wife.

"I'll see you in the morning, then," he said.

Molly hesitated, almost ready to confront him, but then shrugged. It was as clear a dismissal as she'd ever heard.

Feeling hurt he hadn't wanted to stay and talk, she went straight to her room.

Eyeing the connecting door as she prepared for bed, she wished she still shared the room with him. What if the INS required a second inspection? Should she raise that point with him? Would he suggest they share a bed to be able to answer any questions again?

No! He'd compared her to Sabrina, and other women. They'd all wanted something from him. If she was to pique his interest, she had better remember that. Dressing slowly for bed, she tried to envision herself as some fascinating creature who could captivate any man. Maybe because it was so late, but she had difficulty imagining herself as at all interesting. And in a few months she'd be a blimp. No one would find her attractive then. Probably not even a devoted husband—which Kaliq definitely was not.

She wanted his respect, attention—and love.

"Might as well wish for a million dollars," she mused, climbing into her lonely bed. "It's as likely to appear as it would be to have him fall wildly in love with me."

The next week passed at a frantic pace. The meetings with the longshoremen went on day after day, well into the evening hours. Time and again Molly thought the end was in sight, only to have Kaliq balk at a demand or Frank LeBec refuse a point. She was kept busy verifying data and statistics, pulling up examples and extrapolating what different compromises would entail.

Whenever they took a break, Kaliq would close the two of them in his office and rehash the points they'd made or speculate on what the next counterdemand would be. It was exhilarating, but hectic.

By Thursday she was exhausted. And wondering when the contract would be finalized—if ever. The current one expired soon. While the shipping company could fall back on the same standard longshoremen's contract as negotiated with all other shipping lines, Kaliq still wanted better terms.

Molly sat at the negotiating table watching Kaliq trying to anticipate what he might need to shore up a point or add strength to their bid. But more and more as the week went on, she found herself slipping into daydreams.

Had she imagined their night in Washington? Had he really said he wanted their marriage to continue? Would they ever grow close enough to share thoughts and dreams? Or would he always remain aloof, distant? A business arrangement that suited him and made her feel alone and left out?

If the pace of the week was an indication, time would pass swiftly being married to Kaliq, but somehow it wasn't the kind of relationship she had longed for in a marriage.

She wanted the evenings back the way they were their first week together. Quietly sitting together on the low divan. Talking, exploring each other's past. Building routines that would see them through the years.

She even missed Hasim's cooking. A hasty bagel in the morning was the extent of breakfast. Lunches and dinners were catered in the conference room. And she was too tired when she returned to the apartment each night to do anything but fall into bed.

She was getting cranky, she was so tired. Groaning softly, she wondered when she could escape. Why did Kaliq drag the meetings on? LeBec was becoming truculent. Maybe she could suggest an early day tomorrow and let things simmer over the weekend. Returning fresh Monday morning might be a plan beneficial to both sides. Or they could realize they had reached an impasse and do something to kick it loose.

Looking around the table, she realized the men were looking at her expectantly.

What had she missed?

"Molly, you started to say something?" Kaliq said.

Making up her mind, she decided to act. One way or another, she needed to get out of the room. "Actually I'd like to take a short break and speak with you, Kaliq, if you don't mind."

The men rose as she did and she nodded at their manners, sweeping out of the conference room and into Kaliq's office. He followed moments later.

"Yes?" His tone was cool, his manner guarded.

"I'm tired. I'm going home. But before I do, I think you should sign the agreement as stated an hour ago. I don't think LeBec is going to budge. And it incorporates almost everything you wanted. Twice you've put his back up, and sometimes pride is all-important to those men. Even at the risk of losing advantages in a business deal."

He studied her gravely. "I don't think I need you to make my business decisions for me."

"I'm not making any decisions, just offering some advice. Another piece of advice—take a break. Reconvene on Monday. That will give everyone time to really think through the points on the table." She rubbed her forehead, wishing she was already in her bed.

"Are you ill?" Immediately concerned, Kaliq stepped closer and rested his hands on her shoulders.

At the warm touch Molly was hard-pressed not to give in and lean into his strength. She would love nothing better than to be enveloped in his arms, to rest her head against his shoulder and let him take over.

"I'm fine," she replied, standing straight and gently shrugging off his hands. "Just tired. I have a headache.

You don't need me at the table, Kal. I want to go home.''

"I'll take you."

"No. You go back and finish arguing with LeBec."

"Sit. I'll call Hasim." He guided her to a chair. Crossing to the desk, he punched in a number. In only seconds he had instructed Hasim to bring the car. Calling Elise, he asked her to come into the office.

"She'll stay with you until Hasim arrives," Kal said as he lowered the receiver.

"I'm not sick, just tired." But Molly's protest was halfhearted. She liked being cosseted.

Elise was all concern when she hurried into the office. "Are you all right? Nothing wrong with the baby, is there?" she asked, crossing immediately to Molly.

Both Kaliq and Molly looked at her in stunned surprise.

"What? It's not a secret, is it?" Elise asked, seeing their expressions. "Honestly," she said in exasperation, her hands on her hips. "I had five girls and three of them have had babies. Think I don't know the signs?"

"There's nothing wrong with anything except I've got a bit of a headache and am tired," Molly said.

"Not surprising—you've been pushing too hard this week." Elise rounded on Kaliq. "You should take better care of her!"

"Hasim will be here in a short time. If I'm still tied up, will you walk her to the car?" His formal manner did not hide his displeasure at her tone.

"Kaliq! I'm fine," Molly protested. Cosseting was one thing; being treated like an invalid was another.

"Allow me to care for my wife in the manner I think best," he said arrogantly.

She almost groaned at his tone, but meekly nodded and closed her eyes. It felt good to just sit for a moment and do nothing. As soon as she got home, she'd take a nap and when she awoke, she'd feel right as rain.

"Molly?" Kaliq's voice woke her.

"What?"

He leaned over her, shaking her shoulder gently. "You fell asleep. Hasim is here with the car. Let's get you home."

Elise was no longer in the office.

"Okay." She felt a bit disoriented. She had planned to wait until she arrived home to fall asleep. She must be more exhausted than she thought.

Kaliq put his arm around her waist and walked with her to the door.

"I can manage!" she said. The last thing she wanted was for Kaliq to see any weakness.

"I'm sure you can. Indulge me."

Elise's sympathetic gaze met her as they walked through her office. "I hope you feel better real soon, Molly."

"Thanks."

Molly felt as if the eyes of every employee were on them as Kaliq solicitously matched her steps to the elevator.

"Shouldn't you be in the conference room?" she asked crankily. So much fuss embarrassed her.

"I did as you suggested and agreed to the terms. Phil and his staff are finalizing the documents. Once LeBec reviews them to make sure we don't pull a fast one, as he said, then he'll present it to their membership. With any luck we'll have our agreement signed by all parties as early as next Wednesday. Two days before the current contract expires."

Molly was taken aback by his response. He'd agreed to the contract as she'd suggested?

"I'm surprised. I thought you wanted to get him to accept all your terms. I thought for sure the negotiations would go on and on."

The elevator reached the lobby, and Kaliq walked her to the huge glass doors. She saw Kaliq's car double-parked in front of them.

"I'll be fine from here," she said.

"I'm going home with you," Kaliq said as he nodded to Hasim and opened the back door.

"What?" Molly swung around and stared at him. "I'm not sick, Kaliq."

"Neither are you up to your normal healthy self. Permit a husband to indulge himself and see to his wife."

His formality almost made her smile.

"Thank you. But I really just want to go home and lie down for a nap. I'll be fine once I wake up, you'll see."

"Then by all means, let us be on our way."

Molly dozed in the car. When they arrived at the apartment, she stumbled when getting out, glad of Kaliq's arm, which immediately caught her. Without another word, he swept her up into his arms and strode into the building. The doorman opened the door with alacrity.

"Is madam all right?" he asked solicitously.

"She will be soon," Kaliq said, striding to the elevators.

"Put me down," Molly hissed, even as her arm came around his neck.

"When we reach our floor. I can't have you collapsing on me."

"I can walk—I just tripped."

The elevator whisked them to their floor in only seconds. Kaliq seemed content to hold her, ignoring her requests to put her on her feet.

Truth to tell, Molly was secretly thrilled he even thought to carry her. No one had done that since she'd been a baby! And if only she felt better, she knew she'd have cherished the experience. Could she get him to do it again when she did feel better?

Heat stole into her cheeks at the very thought, so Molly gave up and leaned her head against his shoulder. She could almost fall asleep in his arms.

Like she had in Washington.

Kaliq walked into her room and gently set her on the bed.

"Slip out of those things and get into something more comfortable," he suggested.

"I will." She closed her eyes and drifted to the left until she fell back against the mattress. It felt so good to lie down. She'd change her clothes in just a second.

"Molly?"

"Mmm." If she didn't have to open her eyes, she would be all right.

"Come, I'll help you."

Molly tried to sit up when he tugged gently on her arm. Two minutes later her eyes snapped open. He'd removed her suit jacket and was unbuttoning her blouse. She slapped at his hands.

"I can manage!"

"I doubt it." The material parted as he swept it off her shoulders.

"Where's your nightgown?"

"Under the pillow," she said, suddenly wide awake. Conscious of how scantily attired she was, she snatched at the white gown when he pulled it out, and held it against her chest. "I can manage the rest," she said breathlessly.

"With the two of us working together, you can be in bed in seconds," he said, already reaching to unfasten her skirt.

Molly tried to slap away his hand again, but he was already sliding the material over her hips.

"Step out," he ordered when the skirt puddled at her feet.

Kaliq then removed her shoes and reached up to peel off the panty hose.

"Kaliq, stop," she said. She was burning up. If he didn't stop soon, she'd make a huge mistake and throw herself into his arms.

He slowly rose, his gaze roaming over her until he met her eyes. Slowly he smiled, and Molly almost sank back on the bed. Her knees definitely didn't work well under that look.

"I never expected my business-minded personal assistant to indulge herself in such provocative underwear." Reaching out a hand, he ran a fingertip along the top of the lacy edge of her bra, outlining the swell of her breasts.

She was acutely conscious of how scantily attired she was. The brief bikini panties and lacy bra were an indulgence, just as he said. One she had felt safe in luxuriating in because no one else would ever know. Or so she'd thought.

"Kal," she said, afraid of what he'd see if her eyes, but unable to look away.

"Molly." He leaned over and kissed her.

Forgetting everything, she dropped the nightgown and reached up to encircle his neck. His hands were warm and firm against her back as he pressed her against him. She could feel the rough material of his suit, the heat of his body igniting heat in her own. He brought her to life, exhaustion forgotten, as his touch built a craving that had yet to be assuaged.

He pulled back and gazed into her eyes. She almost forgot her own name at the latent desire that shone clearly in his face. They were alone in the apartment, had the rest of the day to themselves. Would he stay? Would he—

Kaliq muttered something under his breath and broke the embrace, reaching down to pick up her nightgown. He slipped it over her head, reached around and unfastened her bra and drew it away.

Molly slipped her arms through the sleeves and felt the soft cotton drift down.

"Into bed," he said, sweeping back the covers. "Now, Molly, before I forget how tired you are and join you."

Her heart pounding in her chest, she looked into his eyes. She longed to invite him to do just that, but dared she?

Before she could say anything, he'd crossed the room to the door. Molly pulled back the covers and slipped beneath them. Closing her eyes, she turned on her side, away from Kaliq, away from the embarrassment of practically throwing herself at him. Such wanton behavior had to be the result of raging hormones from the pregnancy. If he said anything about it, she would excuse it with that.

"Molly," he called softly.

"Mmm?" The brief flash of energy had dissipated. She was almost asleep.

"Another time I won't leave."

Chapter Nine

It was dark when Molly awoke. She lay in bed for a long moment remembering. Had Kaliq said what she thought he'd said just before she fell asleep?

Impossible.

She rose and went to wash her face. Donning a light robe, she wandered out to the living room. Soft lighting illuminated the room. Kaliq reclined on the divan, wearing what Molly considered his desert attire. She paused in the shadows of the hallway for a long moment, watching him. He was reading a book and looked infinitely dear to her. She could imagine him at the doorway to some sumptuous tent, arrogantly surveying all he could see. He had channeled his energies to his family's shipping interests, but she could picture him equally comfortable in the hot Arabian desert defending his land from all invaders.

She must have made some movement or noise, because he suddenly looked right at her.

Rising swiftly, he crossed the room.

"Are you feeling better?" he asked, raising her chin with his finger to look into her eyes.

"Yes, thank you. I'm sorry to flake out on you like that."

"We've had a busy week. Come, I'll have Hasim prepare you something to eat."

"How late is it?" she asked as they walked to the dining room.

"A bit after ten."

"He'll have retired. Don't bother him, Kal. I can find something to eat in the kitchen."

"He has been waiting for you to awake. I believe he has prepared something especially for you."

Ten minutes later Molly sat at the table with a huge bowl of chicken noodle soup and warm rolls before her.

"Is this some kind of universal remedy?" she asked as she dipped her spoon into the bowl. Hasim stood near the doorway watching closely. Kaliq sprawled in his chair, relaxed.

"I believe Elise called to instruct him in its preparation."

"Mmm, it's delicious." She smiled at Hasim and inclined her head in the same manner Kaliq often did. "Thank you, Hasim. It is perfect."

He bowed and left, but she caught a glimpse of the pleased look in his eyes.

"You will have a loyal servant for life," Kaliq said casually. "Tell me the significance of chicken noodle soup."

Molly smiled and ate some more. The warm rolls Hasim prepared went well with the soup. "It's supposed to make you feel better if you're sick. I'm not

sick, just tired, but it is making me feel better. I take
it you don't have such a thing in Manasia?''

Slowly he shook his head. ''Sometimes when I was
a boy and sick, my mother prepared a broth, but not
of chicken. If I become sick, you'll have to remind me
to try this.''

She nodded, unable to imagine the man ever falling
victim to any illness. He'd never had as much as a cold
since she'd known him.

''Should you consider cutting back at work?'' Kaliq
asked.

Molly looked up. ''No! I'm not sick, Kaliq, just
pregnant. This week has been hectic and the hours
long. But I can manage a normal workweek. I can do
my job.''

''We'll see how you feel on Monday.''

''I'll feel fine!''

He smiled at her vehemence and she felt that flutter
in her heart again.

''If you are feeling rested in the morning, I thought
we could go shopping for baby furniture.''

She tilted her head to the side. ''I can't picture you
shopping for furniture.''

''How do you think I acquire new pieces?''

''Wave a hand and order Hasim to go fetch it?''

''And I thought you were an astute businesswoman.
I picked out almost every stick of furniture in this
apartment. I kept nothing from Sabrina's time.''

''I stand corrected. But don't you think it's a bit
early to be buying furniture for the baby? I'm not due
for almost five months.''

''I realize that, but this is a good time. The negotiations are complete. We have a few days before we
leave, so why not now?''

"Leave? Leave for where?"

"Manasia. I phoned my father this afternoon to let him know the negotiations were successfully finished. He wants to meet you. Roeuk told him about you, and he insists we visit. I told him we would leave as soon as the contracts were signed. As long as your doctor says there will be no danger for you. It's a long journey."

She put down her spoon, butterflies suddenly dancing in her stomach. "I don't think I should go," she said. "I'm not sure your parents are going to be thrilled with me as a new daughter-in-law, even a temporary one. Maybe you should go and explain things to them and..." She let her words trail off at the frown on his face.

"Your place is with me. We depart next Friday."

She opened her mouth to protest, then closed it abruptly. She knew that look; she'd seen it often enough over the past five years—stubborn and determined. Her desert warrior would brook no refusal on this issue. And she knew better than to fight it.

The next morning Molly awoke refreshed. The long nap and a solid night's sleep had done wonders. She showered and dressed quickly, trying on several different outfits until she settled on a loose cotton sundress. Her jeans no longer fit comfortably. Brushing her hair, she was pleased to note the circles beneath her eyes were gone. Healthy color glowed in her cheeks.

Kaliq was already at the dining-room table, the remnants of his breakfast in front of him as he sipped coffee and read the paper. How domestic, she thought as she slipped into her seat. She wished she felt more comfortable in the situation.

"Good morning," he said. "You look much better."

"I feel wonderful."

"Up to shopping, then?"

"Always," she replied as Hasim entered carrying a fresh pot of tea.

"Have you decided which room to use as a nursery?" Kaliq asked.

For a moment Molly wanted to tell him she wanted to use *her* room, as it was adjacent to his. But then he'd wonder where she planned to stay, and somehow she hadn't figured out a way to get him to invite her back into his room, to insist she share that big bed.

She shrugged. "Initially the baby can bunk in with me."

Kaliq studied his coffee for a moment, saying nothing. What was he thinking? she wondered. How could she anticipate his needs in business and yet have no clue about what he thought when they were home?

When she had finished eating, Kaliq instructed Hasim to have the car available in thirty minutes.

As they wandered around the infant department in a large store an hour later, Molly realized for the first time what a difference a baby would make in her life. She felt suddenly grateful for the magnitude of Kaliq's gesture in marrying her. No matter what, she'd escape the stigma of being an unwed mother. Not that it mattered that much these days, but it did to her. A direct product of her upbringing, she thought wryly.

Watching Kaliq as he moved purposefully among the furniture, she suspected he would prove to be a good father. He would make sure any child of his felt secure and wanted. And he would teach him well about honesty and honor. She almost stopped in her tracks when she realized how fervently she wished the baby was his. She felt as if she was cheating the man who had offered her so much.

"Something wrong?" he asked as if attuned to her.

She looked up, searching for something that would let her continue on this path.

"No, except..."

He glanced at her and then took her hand, threading his fingers through hers as he pulled her out of the aisle and into a small space near the infant swings. "What is it, Molly?"

She took a deep breath. "Kaliq, I don't think I can go through with this, after all. I'm taking and taking, and you're getting nothing out of this arrangement."

"Buying baby furniture?"

She shook her head, needing to make him understand. "No, not that. This marriage. You'll get your green card and be able to stay in the country. Actually, if you had to leave now, you'd probably have a renewed visa within a few months. And with the negotiations finished..."

"There's the Alderon merger to incorporate into the firm, don't forget."

"I know, but you aren't going to be personally running it. You've already delegated the daily management to Johnson. You can oversee that from Manasia as well as from here. But to be stuck with me and with Chad's baby..." She ran out of words, feeling miserable.

"Ah, I think I see where you are going with this. Do you still long for Chad?"

"Never! He's despicable, and I would never take up with the man again. I feel sorry for his wife and sorry for him and all the joy he'll miss not knowing his child. But I never want to have anything to do with him."

Her sincerity rang clearly. "I loved him once, but he destroyed that love forever. And turned out to be a different man from what I thought he was."

"Then I fail to see the problem."

"It's not fair to you!"

For a long moment Kaliq stared at her. "How is it unfair?"

"You should have someone fresh and free from complications from a previous relationship. Someone who knows how to dress and fit in with galas and opening nights. Someone who will give you lots of babies."

"And you can't?"

She blinked. "I don't know." She was silent for a moment, thinking. "The opening we went to wasn't the disaster I had expected."

"I was speaking of babies."

"Oh." Heat swept through her as she thought of having Kaliq's babies. Of dark-haired infants with black eyes. Her heart rate increased dramatically. "Of course I could, if you really want. But after the night at Roeuk and Megan's, you never said anything more. I thought you had changed your mind."

He raised their linked hands, turning so he could brush his lips across the back of hers. "I did not change my mind."

He looked at her from grave eyes.

"If you had been married before with a child and your husband had died or divorced you, would you expect never to get married again?"

She shook her head.

"Nor would I. If Sabrina and I had had a child and it lived with me, would you come to care for that child?"

"I think I would."

"That's what I think about your baby. I think I will grow to care for that baby as if he or she were my own. Another man may have sired the child, but I will be its father."

Tears welled in her eyes and she tried to absorb the full extent of his meaning.

"Thank you, Kal," she whispered, tightening her grip on his hand.

He brushed back some of her hair, his fingers lingering against her cheek. "Let us have no more doubts, all right?"

She nodded, love overflowing for this strong man. If she had not already tumbled in love with him, his statement would have caused her to do so. Now it just strengthened her feelings. But she knew better than to allow a hint of that love to show. That had not been part of their bargain.

"Then let's go find the best crib we can for our baby," she said calmly.

They examined every crib and listened to the salesclerk explain the various safety features, the benefits of one over another, how easy each model was to assemble. Molly was pleased to discover she and Kal both liked the same one, in cherry wood with turned spindles. They bought a matching cradle and a changing table. Then a whimsical mobile—Kaliq's idea.

Browsing through the bedding, they selected colorful sheets and blankets.

"Not that the baby will need much," she murmured as she piled the bedding in Kaliq's arms.

"You may find things in Manasia you'd like to get," Kaliq said.

"Mmm." She still had doubts and concerns about the impending visit to his country, but she was curious to see his home, to meet his parents and get a new perspective on her husband.

By the time they'd finished shopping, Molly was glad to return to the apartment. She was ready for another nap! Entering, she instantly felt at home. What had changed? Knowing how Kaliq felt toward her baby was one factor. Was hope another? Would someday her husband grow to care for her as he promised to grow to care for her child?

"If we are leaving next week, there is much to do at the office. I will leave you here. Have Hasim clear a space in your room—unless you've changed your mind and wish to use another room for a nursery. When the furniture is delivered, it can go straight into that room."

"I'll keep the cradle in my room for the first few weeks. But maybe we could set up the rest of the furniture in another room."

"I'll be back before dinner."

She turned, loath to have him leave. "I could go in with you," she offered.

Kaliq shook his head. "Rest. Time enough Monday for the hectic pace of the office. Wouldn't you like to go through the things we bought?"

Smiling at the thought of the layette, of the tiny baby clothes and the velvety soft teddy bear Kaliq had also insisted they purchase, Molly hesitated. "Actually I'll wait for you. We can ooh and aah over them together."

He looked at her for a moment, then shook his head slowly. "I'm not a man to ooh and aah over things, Molly."

She laughed. "Okay, Kaliq, then you can just hand them to me, and I'll do enough for both of us. I can't imagine why you said you'd set up the crib. The store would have added installation to the delivery."

"It is what husbands do in America, isn't it? And I am married to an American."

"True. But somehow I can't see you with a screwdriver, on the floor trying to find tab *a* to insert in slot *b*."

He frowned.

She laughed softly again and reached out to pat his arm. "Don't worry, we'll have fun assembling it together. And if we get into a bind, we'll call Hasim."

"I'm sure I can put a crib together, Molly," Kal said stiffly. He drew her closer, his hands lightly gripping her arms. "Or do you doubt my prowess?"

Swallowing hard, Molly shook her head, mesmerized by the fire in his eyes.

Kaliq kissed her quickly, then set her free.

"I'll be home for dinner. Tell Hasim." With that he was gone.

Grateful for the time to rest, Molly took advantage of every moment. She slept in late Sunday and even napped while Kaliq spoke on the phone with Roeuk. By Monday she felt refreshed and ready to face anything.

Just before quitting time Monday afternoon, Kaliq stepped out of his office. "Hasim called—the furniture has arrived. I thought we could leave early and assemble the crib after dinner."

Molly looked up, startled. He seemed as interested in getting things set up for the baby as she was. Slowly she nodded. "I'll just tidy my desk and be ready."

"Hasim will be downstairs in twenty minutes."

They hurried through dinner. As if a treat awaited, instead of an unfamiliar chore.

Molly had chosen a room across the long hall from her own. The baby monitor they'd purchased insured she'd be able to hear the baby no matter where she went, but she liked the thought of having the child close. Once it graduated from the cradle, that is.

Kaliq changed into casual clothes and joined Molly in the room a few minutes after she'd changed. Glancing around, he noted that Hasim had already removed the double bed that had been used for infrequent guests.

"Are you sure you want to do this?" Molly asked, looking at the boxes yet to be opened.

"Certain."

A few minutes later Kaliq had the parts of the crib spread across the floor. It turned out to be a simple task to affix the slide rails, the sides of the crib, the springs. Molly held the ends as he attached the various items. He could almost feel her excitement.

"Did Hasim wash the linen?" he asked as he tightened a screw.

"Yes, everything is ready to be made up. But if I do it this early, everything will be dusty before the baby is born."

"The sheets can be washed again," he said.

She smiled at him, her eyes shining. "Yes, that's true, isn't it? I can't wait to see how it all will look."

He stared at her for a long moment, forgetting the screwdriver he held, forgetting the final steps left in the assembly of the crib. She looked so pretty holding the end of the crib, her eyes full of dreams. He wasn't expecting to feel so much for her. Their relationship had always been business.

But he wanted her. Tightening his grip on the screwdriver, he drew a deep breath. When she looked up at him with that smile, he wanted to throw caution to the wind, sweep her into his arms and kiss her until tomorrow.

"We still have the cradle to do, don't forget," she said happily. "I didn't realize how multitalented you are, Kal. This is great."

Sycophants over the years had tried flattery to get something, but the compliment from Molly was genuine and heartfelt. And touched him as nothing else ever had.

Dragging his gaze away from her, he finished what he was doing.

"If you'll wait, you can help me make up the crib," she said, hurrying from the room. In two minutes she was back, arms piled high with the bedding.

Kal liked working with her. His fingers brushed hers as they smoothed the sheet, brightly covered with circus animals. The bumper pads were tied in place and a fluffy comforter positioned just so.

"Okay, now do the mobile," she ordered, placing the teddy bear in one corner.

Once finished, he could escape to the office, immerse himself in the last-minute details he wanted complete before their trip.

But until then, he was surrounded by the sweet scent of his wife and her enthusiastic delight in the mundane task of making a bed.

When they entered her bedroom to assemble the cradle, Kaliq hesitated in the doorway. There was a feminine feel to the room he'd never noticed before. Her scent filled the air, a frilly nightgown lay where tossed across the pillow, trailing to the floor. Near the dresser was a pair of high heels, one on its side, as if Molly had just kicked them off and let them stay where they landed.

The need to distance himself grew. He was growing too interested in her, too involved. Too caught up in the fantasy of a family life, or what one could be like. Yet nothing had been said of love or lasting commitment. Time enough to reevaluate the situation when he had his green card and the baby was safely delivered.

The cradle looked small when he lifted it onto the supports. Gently pushing it, he could picture a tiny infant snuggled down in it, soothed by the swaying.

He brought his gaze up to Molly. Would the baby look like her?

She smiled and reached out to touch his arm. "Thanks, Kal. This is perfect."

He gripped her arm, drawing her into the circle of his arms, and lowered his face to kiss her. She tasted sweet and warm and womanly. Deepening the kiss, he let the feelings sweep through him, hot and exciting. He wanted her.

Then he stepped back, turned and left the room. He'd been down that road once before. He didn't plan to go that way again. Distance was needed. Distance and distractions.

Molly thought about that kiss on the flight to London. Remembered every caress and embrace she'd shared with Kaliq. For three days—since leaving so abruptly Monday night—he hadn't touched her once. Yet hadn't he said something about wanting to be a daddy to her baby? Didn't that imply a future?

Confused, she tried to find some glimmer of understanding for the complex man sitting beside her. But she felt no closer than the day he'd proposed his wild scheme of a marriage of convenience.

When they returned to New York, she would definitely give Megan a call and see if she could shed some light on how to deal with her husband. It was obvious from the love and devotion between Megan and Roeuk they had found the key. While Molly didn't expect love from Kaliq, maybe she could at least figure out how to draw closer.

Always keeping her own love for him a secret.

He had never made mention of expecting that from her. And after his experience with Sabrina, she knew he didn't have a high opinion of love. But it was hard to resist touching him, soaking up every scrap of time with him, listening to his every word.

From London, they flew to Cairo. Spending the night in a luxurious hotel, Molly saw little of the city; she was too tired and anxious for sleep. Early the next morning they boarded a private jet, which flew them directly to Manasia.

"It's beautiful!" she exclaimed as the plane banked into a turn on its final approach to the airport. The Mediterranean was a deep blue, sugar-white sandy shores edging it. A wide stretch of lush green bordered the beach. In the far distance she could see the edge of the vast Sahara Desert.

"I have always thought so," Kaliq said, leaning close as he, too, gazed from the window.

For him it was home. Would she ever call this place home?

Disembarking, Molly breathed the sweet fragrance in the air. Jasmine, and an unfamiliar scent. But the sudden intense heat caught her unawares, and the glare of the sun seemed relentless.

"Welcome, Your Excellency." A man dressed in the traditional robes of the country greeted Kaliq when he descended the steps. "I have a car over here."

In seconds Molly and Kaliq were ensconced in the cool air-conditioned comfort of a long white limousine. The driver pulled away from the plane and onto one of the major roads.

Molly gazed avidly from the window, trying to see everything. Buildings gleamed sparkling white in the bright sunshine. The roads were smooth and wide with acacia trees lining both sides. Villas were tucked behind high masonry walls, only the tile roofs visible from the street.

As they passed through a shopping district, she was intrigued to see storefronts with names she'd associated with New York and London, side by side with outdoor displays of local merchandise. The people on the sidewalk wore a mixture of colorful robes of all hues and more traditional Western attire. She noticed many of the women wore the all-encompassing black cloaks, which left only their eyes visible.

"Is it required that women wear the cloaks?" she asked, suddenly wondering what she was doing in this country. It seemed so foreign to what she was used to. Exotic and exhilarating, but a bit intimidating.

"Not required. You'll see tourists wandering around in attire they wear at home. Many older more traditional women of the country like to wear them. It gives them a certain anonymity in their dealings with shops and in walking on the streets. Manasia is a safe country. But sometimes visitors can become a bit raucous."

"Would you expect me to wear one?"

"Not if you don't wish to do so. Megan does not when she's here."

Molly continued to stare out the window, wondering what other traditions and customs she would find different.

When the limousine turned between the wide gates of a private estate, she leaned forward, straining to see everything. The villa was lovely—white with soaring columns and a two-tiered veranda around all sides. Gardens with a profusion of blossoms surrounded the house. Beyond, she caught a glimpse of the sea.

"This is my father's home. I have quarters in one wing. We will stay here," Kaliq explained as the limousine pulled to a halt before the wide portico.

"You don't have a place of your own?"

He shook his head. "I've been away from the country more than I've been here in the past twenty years. First to school in England, then to attend to the business in New York. We will have privacy in my quarters."

"I wasn't thinking about that. Just wondering. This is beautiful."

"Come. We'll find my parents and then you can rest."

Exasperated, Molly glared at him. "I'm not tired. I'm too excited. I want to see everything!"

"We'll have time later to see everything," he responded calmly.

"Even spend a night or two on the desert?" she asked as they entered the cool foyer.

He inclined his head. "If that is what you wish."

Molly frowned.

Kaliq's parents were austere and reserved. Molly watched them greet their son with quiet dignity and then turn to her. She spoke when spoken to, feeling intimidated and uncomfortable. Gratefully she acqui-

esced to Kaliq's suggestion that they seek their rooms
to change after traveling.

Her feeling of being totally out of place faded when
she saw their rooms. They were warm and inviting.
High ceilings gave the illusion that they were larger
than their actual size. The outside wall was entirely
glass, with French doors that opened to a veranda. Had
this been the model for the apartment in New York?

The windows overlooked the garden and the sea beyond. She spotted a walkway, partially hidden by tow-
ering shrubs that led to the beach.

"It's beautiful," she said sincerely, crossing to the
windows to gaze at the view. "I want to walk beside
the Mediterranean. Go swimming." She spun around.
"I can't go swimming—I'd feel like a beached whale,
plus, I don't have a suit that will fit."

"Whales don't come as small as you. At this stage
it's hard to even tell you are pregnant. And lack of a
suit is not a problem. Tomorrow we can go shopping.
We'll find something that will fit."

"No, I don't need to go swimming." She gave a
quick longing glance at the sea, then turned back, her
mind made up. No use repining about something she
chose to forego. Maybe on another visit.

If there was ever another visit.

What if his father didn't like her? What if he didn't
want his son married to another foreigner? What if Kaliq realized he'd made a mistake? Was the reason for
his distracted air that he was already thinking of ways
to end their marriage? Her heart sank. Just when she
thought they were drawing closer, he was pulling away.

He crossed the room and tilted her chin up with a
finger, gazing down into her eyes. Molly caught her

breath, longing to gaze into his eyes for the rest of her life.

"We will go shopping tomorrow. Today, rest. I will visit with my parents while you do so. Tonight we'll dine on the veranda and enjoy the scents and sounds of my home."

"With your parents?" She was no good at small talk. What would she find to discuss during dinner?

"Tonight is for us alone. You'll have plenty of time in the days ahead to get to know my mother and father."

She nodded, her heart sinking again. Coming had been a mistake. Yet how could she have refused?

Molly walked out onto the wide veranda once Kaliq had left and leaned on the wide railing. The sea looked cool and inviting and such a deep blue. She felt she'd obtained a respite. Tomorrow would be time enough to figure out what to talk about with Kaliq's formidable parents. Tonight it would be just the two of them— with no pressures from work, no distractions, nothing to stop Kaliq from giving her his undivided attention, and who knows where that might lead.

Slowly Molly began to smile.

Two days later Molly wasn't smiling. She leaned against the railing and glared at the sea. Nothing was going as she had thought it would. Who would have expected Kaliq to be tied up so much with business? Didn't his father trust him? They'd been behind closed doors for hours every day. And tonight there was a reception. An event to welcome home their son and his new bride.

Only she didn't feel welcome. Kaliq was more distant than ever. Waiting until she was asleep before coming to bed, he was gone before she awoke in the morning. And they were never alone. His manners were excellent, but so formal. What was going on?

Had being at his home changed his mind? Was he now regretting his hasty marriage to another foreigner? Did he wish to end their agreement and seek true companionship among the women of his homeland?

Restless, she pushed away from the railing and headed down the stairs to the garden. Garden was a misnomer. Estate would be more like it, she thought as she reached the area. It was huge, easily more than ten acres. Winding her way along the sandy pathway, she touched the shrubbery lining the walkway. It grew tall enough to be used in a maze. Alcoves were set every dozen feet with stone benches and small gurgling fountains. Sitting on one for a moment, she tried to let the soothing sound of the water calm her nerves.

No use. She jumped up and continued walking toward the beach. There was an ornamental gate—for show, not security. It was only latched, not locked. She lifted the lever and stepped onto the pristine sand. Not a soul had used the beach since she arrived. It was private to the family and none of them seemed as enamored with it as she was.

Feeling free for a moment, she ran lightly across the sand until her sandals were drenched with the lapping water. Warm and soft, it seemed to caress her feet. Splashing as she walked, she headed along the edge. She wished Kaliq had joined her, but he was once again tied up with his father.

And if she could be at ease with his mother, maybe she wouldn't feel so much like an odd man out. But Sarianna bin Shalik spoke English hesitantly. And slowly. Honored she'd even make the effort, Molly still felt it was a chore and she hated to put the woman through it. They had little in common. Kaliq's mother had no interest in business.

After two days Molly knew the various people who lived in the large house and had even met many of the ministers and other cabinet officials who frequented the place.

Molly had known Roeuk bin Shalik was the titular head of the principality but she hadn't realized Mohammad bin Shaliq, Kaliq's father, was his nephew's most important adviser and constantly dealt with affairs of state. Mohammad's secretary, Jarin Moktomad, seemed a part of the household. The man did not appear to approve of her. Had he approved of Sabrina? Or was he just opposed to the son of his employer marrying a foreign—

"Molly!"

She turned and her heart caught, skipped, raced.

Kaliq wore the loose white trousers he often wore at the apartment. The shirt billowed in the light breeze that danced across the water. She waited, watching him approach, her heart in her throat. He was so gorgeous it was all she could do to keep herself from dashing down the beach and throwing herself into his arms, demanding that he love her as much as she loved him.

"Free for a while?" she asked as he drew near. She knew her place in the scheme of things. Kaliq wasn't looking for love.

He was barefoot, and just the site of his bare feet set her nerves atingle.

"Free until it's time to get ready for the reception." He looked across the sea. "We could go sailing one day if you wish."

"Tomorrow? That would be great. But it's also fun to walk along the beach. I haven't seen any shells."

"The sands are raked every few days. Until there is another storm, I doubt you'll find any."

Imagine, they raked the sand. No wonder the wide expanse was so pristine.

"I thought you might be with my mother," he said as they began walking in the direction Molly had been heading.

"It seems awkward for her to speak English." Had she heard a note of censure? Or just gentle inquiry?

"She likes the chance to practice. Is it too difficult to understand her?"

"Oh, no! She has a beautiful accent, very British and all. Like yours." She hesitated a moment.

"Ah, but there is something."

"What could we talk about, Kal? You know I'm not good at small talk, and she and I have nothing in common."

"You can discuss children. She has raised several and would be delighted to offer suggestions. She hesitates to intrude, however."

Molly swung around and stared at him. "You told them about the baby?"

Chapter Ten

Kaliq nodded. "It is not something that can be kept a secret, you know."

"What did they say? Are they horrified? Oh, Kaliq, I wish you had waited until after we returned home."

"They are my parents, Molly. I could not in honor keep such an event from them. Besides, my mother guessed."

"What did they say?"

He drew a deep breath, remembering the scene with his father. He would not like to repeat such an afternoon, but what was done was done. "My mother loves babies. She will be delighted."

"Will be? When? Obviously not now."

"Understand, they are concerned because the baby is not mine."

"I bet your father threw a fit."

He smiled slightly and shook his head. "Not precisely. He is not one given to throwing fits." But his temper was not something Kaliq liked to run up against often.

"You know what I mean," she said impatiently. "I bet they are furious. Do they want me to leave?"

"Molly, they are hosting a reception tonight for the express purpose of introducing you to our friends and other family members. How could they want you to leave?"

"I feel funny seeing them again. I bet they wish the baby was yours."

"Yes, they do. I won't hide that from you."

"Well, I don't blame them, I wish—" She stopped abruptly and looked horrified.

"What? Is something wrong?" Without thought, he reached for her, drawing her into his embrace. "What is it, Molly?"

"Nothing. The baby gave an odd kick, that's all."

"Ah. Can I feel him kick?"

"What?" Molly pushed against his chest, but Kaliq refused to release her. He liked holding Molly. Liked being with her. These last two days couldn't have been easy for her left alone so much, but his father wanted to be brought up to speed on the various enterprises in America. And both evenings when he'd retired, she'd already been sound asleep. Not that he wanted to lead her on. He was not planning to give his heart to anyone. Especially a woman who married him for convenience.

Slowly she turned in his embrace and took one of his hands, pressing it against the slight swelling of her abdomen. Kaliq was aware of the warmth beneath his palm, of her scent filling his senses, of her hair blowing against his cheek when he leaned closer. "It could be a girl," she said.

Then, a slight movement beneath his palm.

"There, did you feel that?" she asked.

Touched beyond belief, he nodded and held still, longing to feel that flutter of life again. Twice more he felt something.

"So he's going to be a soccer player."

"Or ballet dancer," she murmured, resting against his chest.

"This is a special gift you have given me, Molly. I thank you."

"No, Kaliq, you've given me a special gift. One for which I will always be grateful."

He stepped back, annoyed at her sentiments. "I don't want your gratitude," he said sharply.

She looked at him for a long moment, then nodded. "Very well," she said stiffly. She hesitated a moment, then turned to retrace her steps. "I'm feeling tired and think I should rest this afternoon. We'll be up late tonight."

Kaliq stood and watched her walk back toward the villa. Her head was high and her shoulders back, but he had the feeling she was not as confident as she appeared. For a long moment he watched her walk away. She had not asked him to accompany her, had not sought his company.

Was that to be the way of their marriage? Parallel lives, never connecting, never intersecting?

Molly pushed through the gate and headed up the sandy path. Flouncing down on one of the benches, she glared at the shrubbery opposite. Things were not going well and she hadn't a clue what to do about it.

"Madam?"

Turning, she saw Jarin.

"Hello."

"I saw you come in from a walk on the beach. You left Kaliq there."

"Yes." She would not air dirty laundry before anyone—especially an aide to Kal's father. She already knew his father didn't approve. No sense feeding that disapproval.

"Kaliq is His Excellency's oldest son. He is heir to his father's holdings. His place will be here in Manasia when His Excellency dies. While that may not be for many years, Kaliq will need the help and support of his family."

Molly nodded. "Do you think I would not be willing to move here when that time comes?"

"You know nothing about our country, our customs, our traditions. I suspect you simply saw a wealthy man, captivated him with your wiles and beguiled him into marriage. This is not what his father wished for him. But it is not too late to change things. Dissolve this absurd marriage and I'll see that you have ample funds to live the kind of life you hoped to live with Kaliq—better, for you will not be restricted by our customs."

"There's not enough money in the world," she said scornfully.

"You prefer the prestige of being married to him, is that it? Because of his place in our society, as well as the wealth."

"No! You forget, in my country we don't go in for royalty and all that. He's just a businessman there. And money only buys things. I'm not a thing and I'm not interested in money. If his father thought to buy me off, too bad. I'm not leaving."

"We can make things very uncomfortable for you."

Molly had had enough. She leaped to her feet, placed her hands on her hips and glared at him.

"Doesn't matter. It's Kaliq who matters. If he tells me to leave, I will. But I won't go unless he's the one to tell me!"

"I did not say I come from his father. Did you ever consider that I might be here from Kaliq directly?" Jarin asked slowly.

"Ha! If Kaliq didn't like the arrangement, he'd let me know in no uncertain terms. He's the one who proposed this crazy marriage. I expect he will tell me directly if he tires of it. He doesn't need some gofer to do that." But the doubts built. Hadn't she noticed he'd pulled away in the last few days? Was he regretting their hasty alliance? Had he sought to avoid a scene by sending Jarin?

"A besotted woman thinks she can wrap a man around her finger. Better take the offer while it's still available, or you'll be out with nothing."

"Besotted!" She wanted to scream with frustration. "I may love the man, but I'm not besotted. He isn't perfect. He's dictatorial, arrogant and always ordering things to suit him. Like this marriage."

"Love?" Jarin sounded perplexed. "What does that have to do with marriage? Kaliq needs a woman of his own country to give him strong sons, to insure the line."

"I know enough about love to know he also needs someone on his side, someone who cares about him and what he's thinking and feeling, and not for some succession thing. And if he wants sons, I can give them to him. He doesn't need a woman just because of her place of birth. He had his chance to meet someone here, yet he chose me. So you just march inside and let his father know I'm not leaving unless Kaliq tells me to!"

Jarin hesitated a moment, then calmly inclined his head. "As you wish."

Furious, Molly watched him walk away as if he had not a care in the world. Had he come from Kaliq? Had being in his own country changed Kaliq's mind about staying with her? He had made no moves to increase their intimacy—didn't that prove he was losing interest?

She turned and headed back toward the beach, then saw Kaliq when she reached the gate. Hoping for a moment to calm her nerves, she waited for him, her anger growing as he took his time. Anger and suspicions that maybe Jarin had been telling the truth. Maybe he *had* come from Kaliq.

"I want to speak to you!" she said when he drew close.

"About?"

Kaliq paused by the gate and studied Molly. She knew she was flushed with the anger that threatened to overwhelm her. But that couldn't be helped. She needed answers now.

"About an attempted bribe to end our marriage."

"What are you talking about?" He seemed surprised at her announcement. "Who has mentioned a bribe? Or even hinted at ending the marriage?"

"Your father's secretary. He suggested he came from you, but I don't believe him. At least, I don't think I do. He said you wanted to end our marriage and would give me lots of money to go."

"Ah. And your response?" Kaliq waited politely, his gaze never leaving hers.

"I told him I wasn't for sale. If you wish to end this relationship, you come right out and tell me. Otherwise, it sticks!" Without waiting for a response, she whirled around and almost ran to the stairs leading to their balcony.

She was almost shaking with nerves. Had she made another mistake, a worse one than with Chad? The emotion she felt for that man had faded, seemed paltry compared to the intensity of her love for Kaliq. But her track record wasn't great with men. Had she misread the signs, trying to convince herself that Kaliq wanted her as much as she wanted him?

Several hours later Molly twisted this way and that as she looked at herself in the mirror, wondering if she should wear the dress or not. It had looked elegant and sophisticated in New York. But with the heightened modesty prevalent among the women she'd met since arriving in Manasia, she wondered if it was too daring.

The gown brushed her ankles as she walked, the soft pale yellow chiffon falling from the clip at her left shoulder. The right was bare. Both arms were bare and lightly tanned from her days on the beach. The loose-fitting garment hid all signs of her pregnancy, and looked feminine and alluring.

Tilting her head slightly, she narrowed her eyes. Alluring? Would Kaliq find her alluring? Slowly she practiced a smile. She'd loved to be sultry and sexy, mysterious and intriguing. But then, she sighed. She looked like she always did—just plain old Molly Larkin all dressed up for the ball.

Kaliq knocked on the partially open door. He stepped inside, looking splendid in the white dinner jacket. His dark hair gleamed in the light. For a moment Molly thought a matching light gleamed in his eyes. But she must have been imagining it. Flustered from her outburst by the gate, she was unsure how to greet him. He had not confirmed nor denied his involvement with the bribe. And despite her fine words about wanting to know, she hesitated to push the issue. What would she do if he walked away? Trying to ignore the rapid beat of her heart, she raised her chin. She would not give way to fear. What happened, happened, and she would just have to deal with it.

"Will this do?" she asked. "It's not too daring, is it?" *Do you wish to end our marriage?*

He shook his head. "My mother buys her gowns in Paris. A direct influence of her sister-in-law, Roeuk's mother. The party will be like any other you've attended. Most of the guests speak English and will do so in your presence."

"I guess I'm ready, then," she muttered, touching her hair, nervous with him watching her. How she wished Kaliq had firmly denied any involvement in the bribe. She wished he'd reaffirm his commitment to their marriage. Say something to end this uncertainty.

Instead of attending the reception, she wished he'd sweep her into his arms and carry her off to a romantic tent in the desert. She would love to spend the evening watching the sun set over the dunes, feel the dry clear air against her skin. Make love beneath a blanket of brilliant stars.

It was only a dream. Tonight she had to endure yet another gathering where she'd feel insecure and uncertain. And Kaliq did nothing to help!

"You look lovely."

The warmth of his compliment surprised her. Meeting his eyes in the mirror, she smiled shyly. "Thank you."

"Shall we?" Kaliq offered his hand and Molly slipped hers into it. The heat from his palm warmed hers. Taking a deep breath, she grew determined to do her very best to not let Kaliq down. He'd done so much for her she wanted to make sure he never regretted it.

If she could not have his love, she would make sure she kept his respect!

Kaliq scanned the ballroom. He didn't see Molly and wondered where she'd gotten to. His mother had invited half the country, he thought in wry amusement. And he felt as if he'd talked to everyone present. Many had met Molly and then expressed their views of his marrying another foreigner. Most of them favorable. Not that it mattered. He would choose his own wife.

Once again he searched the room. She was not anywhere to be seen. Maybe she went outside. Slowly he made his way to the veranda. Couples walked in the evening coolness, and a few had gathered in a small group, sharing laughter and conversation.

"Looking for your bride?" his cousin Emil asked.

"Have you seen her?"

Emil nodded toward the garden. "She and Calache bin Molou walked in that direction a few moments ago. She is very unlike Sabrina, cousin."

Kaliq looked at him. "To the good or bad?"

"Much to the good. I wish you all happiness."

Kaliq nodded and headed in the direction Emil had indicated. The path looked deserted. At the intersection with another, he heard voices. Slowly he turned, drawing closer. He could hear them clearly before he could see them.

"I knew Sabrina well. Are you as enchanting and generous as she?"

"What does that mean?" Molly asked.

"She was, shall we say, generous with her favors. I wonder if Kaliq's present wife is as generous."

Kaliq stopped dead, anger slowly building. How dare Calache make such a remark to his wife! Kaliq's hands fisted and he began to move forward. He'd make the man regret he ever entertained such a thought, much less voiced it!

But Molly's voice stopped him.

"I've got news for you, buster. Sabrina and I are nothing alike. So take your hands off me before I bop you one."

"I like fire in a woman."

"Yes, well, so does Kaliq. And I suspect he is not one to share. Not that I would ever be tempted. I love my husband, and I find every other man on the planet only a pale imitation! If you want to walk out of here, take a hike now before the palace guards show up and throw you in prison!"

"A misunderstanding. My apologies." Calache moved away.

"Actually we don't have palace guards," Kaliq said, stepping around the curve in the path. Kaliq let out his pent-up breath as he looked at his wife. His heart began to beat rapidly.

"Hi, Kaliq," she said. He liked the flustered look about her. Gone was the cool serene personal assistant he was used to seeing every day. Before him stood a woman with sparkling eyes and wearing a dress designed to drive a man mad.

"I couldn't help overhearing your altercation with Calache."

"Honestly, I can't believe the man thought I'd want to dally in the garden with him. What an ego." She tried to brush past Kaliq. "Time to return to the party, I guess."

"In a moment. I heard you tell him you loved me."

She studied one of the flowering bushes highlighted by the garden lights. "Mmm."

He reached out and tilted her chin until she looked up and met his gaze.

"Is it true, Molly?"

She swallowed. He watched the movement of her throat and thought how he'd like to kiss her there.

"Yes, it's true. But I won't let it change anything. I remember the terms of our agreement."

"Ah." He was silent a long moment, staring into her eyes, watching them change from defiant to apprehensive.

"That is, if you still want to stay married," she said slowly.

"Why wouldn't I?"

"I don't know. Jarin had a point. Others probably think I'm like Sabrina—like that man did." She raised her chin. "But I'm not!"

"No, Molly, you are not."

"So we carry on?" She held her breath. *Please say yes!*

"Actually a good negotiator knows when to change things," he murmured, drawing her into his arms. "I believe it's time to change the terms of our marriage agreement."

"You do?" Her eyes grew wide. "How?"

"I want to make it real."

"Oh," was all she had time to say before his mouth came down on hers.

Kaliq felt the blood sing in his veins. *She loves me.* It was more than he expected or deserved.

Long moments later the sound of voices intruded. Kaliq broke the kiss, grabbed her hand and headed away from the house.

"That's the problem with parties—there's no privacy."

Molly kept pace, her hand gripping his. When they reached the gate, Kaliq urged her through to the pristine white sand.

"Are you sure, Kaliq? I would stay with no strings."

He ran his finger along her cheek, beneath her jaw, savoring the silky texture of her skin. His longing to make her his grew with each passing moment.

"I think I'd like strings, and ties and chains if they kept you with me forever."

She smiled and he smiled back, feeling the relief flow through him.

"I love you, Molly bin Shalik. I think I realized it the day in the department store when you worried about what I was getting out of our arrangement. I think that is the first time anyone ever worried about my benefits. I know it in my heart and soul—you are all I need and want. And whether you give me fine strong sons or not, it won't matter. You will be all I need for the rest of my life."

"Oh, Kaliq!" She flung herself into his arms, encircling his neck with hers and hugging him tightly. "I love you so much. I thought you only married me for expediency, and I vowed I would never give you a reason to regret it. But I think I've loved you for ages. I knew for sure when we stayed at Roeuk's."

He relished the sensation of her soft body against the length of his. "I thought you felt gratitude."

She shook her head. "I do, but that's only part of it. Mostly I love you."

"Overbearing and a bit arrogant as I am?" he murmured, his lips trailing kissed along her sweet skin.

She nodded. "You on a bad day are better than any other man in the world on his best day," she whispered. "But are you sure? I don't want to cause a problem in your family."

"My mother already loves you. My father shall come around. Especially when he sees how happy you make me. But I'm not here to talk about them, only about us. Shall we steal away tonight, lose ourselves in the wide expanse of the Sahara and have that honeymoon Elise has been lecturing me about?"

She gave a gurgle of laughter. "I can't see Elise lecturing anyone, especially you!"

"Ah, perhaps they were more like strong hints. But you didn't answer my question."

Molly's eyes drifted shut. "I would love nothing better."

Kaliq was not a man to resist a blatant invitation. His mouth closed over hers again and he kissed his wife with all the love in his heart. Tomorrow he'd show her the beauty of the desert. They'd spend a few weeks alone truly beginning their lives together. And when it was time, they'd return to their home in New York stronger than ever in their marriage—because of the endless ties of love.

Epilogue

"It's a girl," the doctor said as the lusty cries filled the birthing room.

"We have a daughter," Kaliq said with satisfaction.

Molly promptly burst into tears. She clung to her husband's hand and tried to smile through the tears. "Is she all right?" she asked.

"Looks perfect," the doctor said, laying the baby on Molly's stomach. Kaliq reached out to run a finger down her cheek, and she stopped crying, her wide infant eyes turning to him.

"She's beautiful," he murmured. "Just like her mother."

Molly blinked furiously, trying to see clearly. "Looks tiny and red and—"

"Hush, love. She will be as beautiful as you." Kaliq leaned over to kiss her, his fingers lacing through hers. "Or almost. I doubt anyone will ever be that lovely."

Molly smiled and tightened her grip. "I love you," she said.

"I love you and Sarianna Alicia."

"Is that what we will call her?"

"Unless you prefer another name."

"We will name our next daughter for my mother. My parents are anxious for us to visit so they can see Alicia and you."

"I'm glad they've accepted me."

"Accepted? Darling, they love you for yourself and because you've made me so happy.

"Shall we go as soon as you and our daughter are ready, so we can show her off."

"Whatever you say," Molly said, fascinated by the baby who was now looking around as if taking in the brand-new world she had just entered.

"We'll clean her up and bring her to you in a few minutes," the nurse said briskly, wrapping a warm blanket around the infant and whisking her away.

"Is this new docility going to continue?" Kaliq asked to distract her when he saw the look on her face at the departure of her new daughter.

"What?" She looked at him. "What docility?"

"Whatever I say?"

"That's temporary, until I'm in fighting shape again."

"But we rarely fight," he said, smiling in memory of some of the terrific *discussions* they'd had. And the making up afterward.

She laughed and reached up to pull him closer.

"I love you, Kaliq. You've made my life perfect."

"Ah, Molly, only Allah is perfect. But you and I together come pretty damn close!"

* * * * *

VIRGIN BRIDES

**Join
Silhouette Romance
as the New Year brings new
virgin brides down the aisle!**

On Sale December 1999
THE BRIDAL BARGAIN
by Stella Bagwell (SR #1414)

On Sale February 2000
WAITING FOR THE WEDDING
by Carla Cassidy (SR #1426)

On Sale April 2000
HIS WILD YOUNG BRIDE
by Donna Clayton (SR #1441)

Watch for more **Virgin Brides** stories from
your favorite authors later in 2000!

VIRGIN BRIDES
only from

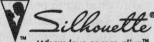

Silhouette®
Where love comes alive™

Available at your favorite retail outlet.

Visit us at www.romance.net

SRVB00

SILHOUETTE'S 20TH ANNIVERSARY CONTEST
OFFICIAL RULES
NO PURCHASE NECESSARY TO ENTER

1. To enter, follow directions published in the offer to which you are responding. Contest begins 1/1/00 and ends on 8/24/00 (the "Promotion Period"). Method of entry may vary. Mailed entries must be postmarked by 8/24/00, and received by 8/31/00.

2. During the Promotion Period, the Contest may be presented via the Internet. Entry via the Internet may be restricted to residents of certain geographic areas that are disclosed on the Web site. To enter via the Internet, if you are a resident of a geographic area in which Internet entry is permissible, follow the directions displayed on-line, including typing your essay of 100 words or fewer telling us "Where In The World Your Love Will Come Alive." On-line entries must be received by 11:59 p.m. Eastern Standard time on 8/24/00. Limit one e-mail entry per person, household and e-mail address per day, per presentation. If you are a resident of a geographic area in which entry via the Internet is permissible, you may, in lieu of submitting an entry on-line, enter by mail, by hand-printing your name, address, telephone number and contest number/name on an 8"x 11" plain piece of paper and telling us in 100 words or fewer "Where In The World Your Love Will Come Alive," and mailing via first-class mail to: Silhouette 20th Anniversary Contest, (in the U.S.) P.O. Box 9069, Buffalo, NY 14269-9069; (In Canada) P.O. Box 637, Fort Erie, Ontario, Canada L2A 5X3. Limit one 8"x 11" mailed entry per person, household and e-mail address per day. On-line and/or 8"x 11" mailed entries received from persons residing in geographic areas in which Internet entry is not permissible will be disqualified. No liability is assumed for lost, late, incomplete, inaccurate, nondelivered or misdirected mail, or misdirected e-mail, for technical, hardware or software failures of any kind, lost or unavailable network connection, or failed, incomplete, garbled or delayed computer transmission or any human error which may occur in the receipt or processing of the entries in the contest.

3. Essays will be judged by a panel of members of the Silhouette editorial and marketing staff based on the following criteria:

   Sincerity (believability, credibility)—50%

   Originality (freshness, creativity)—30%

   Aptness (appropriateness to contest ideas)—20%

   Purchase or acceptance of a product offer does not improve your chances of winning. In the event of a tie, duplicate prizes will be awarded.

4. All entries become the property of Harlequin Enterprises Ltd., and will not be returned. Winner will be determined no later than 10/31/00 and will be notified by mail. Grand Prize winner will be required to sign and return Affidavit of Eligibility within 15 days of receipt of notification. Noncompliance within the time period may result in disqualification and an alternative winner may be selected. All municipal, provincial, federal, state and local laws and regulations apply. Contest open only to residents of the U.S. and Canada who are 18 years of age or older, and is void wherever prohibited by law. Internet entry is restricted solely to residents of those geographical areas in which Internet entry is permissible. Employees of Torstar Corp., their affiliates, agents and members of their immediate families are not eligible. Taxes on the prizes are the sole responsibility of winners. Entry and acceptance of any prize offered constitutes permission to use winner's name, photograph or other likeness for the purposes of advertising, trade and promotion on behalf of Torstar Corp. without further compensation to the winner, unless prohibited by law. Torstar Corp and D.L. Blair, Inc., their parents, affiliates and subsidiaries, are not responsible for errors in printing or electronic presentation of contest or entries. In the event of printing or other errors which may result in unintended prize values or duplication of prizes, all affected contest materials or entries shall be null and void. If for any reason the Internet portion of the contest is not capable of running as planned, including infection by computer virus, bugs, tampering, unauthorized intervention, fraud, technical failures, or any other causes beyond the control of Torstar Corp. which corrupt or affect the administration, secrecy, fairness, integrity or proper conduct of the contest, Torstar Corp. reserves the right, at its sole discretion, to disqualify any individual who tampers with the entry process and to cancel, terminate, modify or suspend the contest or the Internet portion thereof. In the event of a dispute regarding an on-line entry, the entry will be deemed submitted by the authorized holder of the e-mail account submitted at the time of entry. Authorized account holder is defined as the natural person who is assigned to an e-mail address by an Internet access provider, on-line service provider or other organization that is responsible for arranging e-mail address for the domain associated with the submitted e-mail address.

5. Prizes: Grand Prize—a $10,000 vacation to anywhere in the world. Travelers (at least one must be 18 years of age or older) or parent or guardian if one traveler is a minor, must sign and return a Release of Liability prior to departure. Travel must be completed by December 31, 2001, and is subject to space and accommodations availability. Two hundred (200) Second Prizes—a two-book limited edition autographed collector set from one of the Silhouette Anniversary authors: Nora Roberts, Diana Palmer, Linda Howard or Annette Broadrick (value $10.00 each set). All prizes are valued in U.S. dollars.

6. For a list of winners (available after 10/31/00), send a self-addressed, stamped envelope to: Harlequin Silhouette 20th Anniversary Winners, P.O. Box 4200, Blair, NE 68009-4200.

Contest sponsored by Torstar Corp., P.O. Box 9042, Buffalo, NY 14269-9042.

PS20RULES

ENTER FOR A CHANCE TO WIN*

Silhouette's 20th Anniversary Contest

Tell Us Where in the World You Would Like *Your* Love To Come Alive... And We'll Send the Lucky Winner There!

Silhouette wants to take you wherever your happy ending can come true.

Here's how to enter: Tell us, in 100 words or less, where you want to go to make your love come alive!

In addition to the grand prize, there will be 200 runner-up prizes, collector's-edition book sets autographed by one of the Silhouette anniversary authors: **Nora Roberts, Diana Palmer, Linda Howard** or **Annette Broadrick.**

DON'T MISS YOUR CHANCE TO WIN! ENTER NOW! No Purchase Necessary

Silhouette®
Where love comes alive™

Name:

Address:

City: State/Province:

Zip/Postal Code:

Mail to Harlequin Books: **In the U.S.:** P.O. Box 9069, Buffalo, NY 14269-9069; **In Canada:** P.O. Box 637, Fort Erie, Ontario, L4A 5X3